Poi Son

KIM ROBERTS

Copyright © 2013
Copyright © Kim Roberts

All rights reserved, including the right to reproduce this work
In any form whatsoever without permission in writing from the publisher,
Except for brief passages in connection with a review.

ISBN 978-0-9885868-3-3

Dedication

To Blain and all the boy-dogs with whom I've shared this life.

Acknowledgements

Special thanks to Marlene Thomasson, Barb Aue,
and Momi Palmieri for their editing efforts.
Anything that doesn't ring true is mine.

Poison: 1. a substance with an inherent property that tends to destroy life or impair health. 2. something harmful or pernicious, as to happiness or well-being: *the poison of slander.* 3. *Slang.* any variety of alcoholic liquor: *Name your poison!* 4. to administer poison (to a person or animal). 5. to kill or injure with or as if with poison. 6. to put poison into or upon; saturate with poison: *to poison food.* 7. To ruin, vitiate, or corrupt: *Hatred had poisoned his mind.*

Webster's Encyclopedic Unabridged
Dictionary of the English Language

Chapter One

That morning when I woke up, I didn't know I'd lose my job, go to the place of my biggest embarrassment, and end up in bed with my ex-husband.

Really, who could see all that coming?

It was the kind of Maui day where I would have shot my partner, but I didn't feel like doing the paperwork. Don't get me wrong, I'm not lazy. Together we had chased a huge local dude, maybe Tongan or Samoan, wearing a red banana hammock as a swimsuit with a matching doo-rag as a hat, across the beach. I'm not a runner, neither is my partner, so the big guy maintained his lead until he ran down the dock.

"Stop! You're under arrest!" Not only did I witness the crime—the shoplifting of the marshmallows—but also had to yell that message in order to get him for evading once I caught him. Having just graduated from the reserve academy, I knew the law. I just hoped I'd actually catch him.

So, lickety-split, the big guy jammed out onto the concrete dock and I was thinking, *Dude, haven't you ever heard of that long walk on a short dock-thing?*

I didn't have time to verbalize it, because in front of me my partner ripped around the corner onto the dock, lost his footing, and sprawled face first in my path.

By then I had one hand on my gun—still in the holster mind you—and I was having bad thoughts. Thoughts like, "Why me? Can I call it self-defense if I shoot him? Does my ass look fat in these shorts?"

And the ever-present, "I wonder where I could get just one piece of wedding cake." I love wedding cake. In fact, I think that's why I got married once, a long time ago.

Of course, none of this was happening in a vacuum. The summer weekend had drawn the usual variety of Lahaina tourists and locals to Mala Wharf. A crowd followed the chase and clustered around us. They offered various forms of support to me, like "Shoot him!" They also advised the perp, "Jump!" And when they saw him from behind, one woman screamed, "Oh, dear God, he's wearing a T-back!"

I have several basic truths in life. The latest has to do with thongs. Don't wear 'em, don't want to see fat guys wearing 'em.

It applied now, but so did another, one I had learned while in the law enforcement academy. It came from a book with the creepy title, *On Killing*. It contends there are three kinds of people: Sheep, sheepdogs and wolves. Most people are sheep, munching, mating and trundling along the meandering trail of life. A few—like my five sisters and me—are sheepdogs; mostly law enforcement or military, we protect the sheep. Then there are the wolves—those who prey on the sheep and the sheep dogs.

As I eye-balled the situation in slow-mo, the sheep suddenly surrounded me—the sheep dog—looking into the crazed gaze of a potential wolf. This was not how it was supposed to go. I looked at my partner. As he gathered all four feet under himself, we all saw the big "suspect" shove the marshmallows into his beach bag where I couldn't see his hands. I thought, *Crap, if he has a gun, he'll shoot at me and into my flock of sheep!*

"Get back, everybody! Get back!" I yelled as I popped the snaps on my holster and did a quick draw, got both hands on the gun, and aimed. That got his attention.

"This is racial profiling, you Aryan Amazon!" He still had one hand in the bag, the other pointed at me with his accusation.

Nice alliteration, and it drew a few chuckles from the crowd, but it still pissed me off. I'm a five-foot ten, blonde who is *chop suey* in heritage. I'm a quarter German from my dad's side and a quarter Native American from my mom, with a whole bunch of other stuff mixed in like spices in meatloaf.

In Hawai'i, I wasn't even up to what's called *hapa haole*, or half white. In all areas, I get enough guff without this twerp's opinion. As far as I'm concerned, my family alone allows me to be pissed most of the time, not that I need a reason. I mean really, who names six girls "love"—each in a different language—might as well tape a sign on my back that says, "Kick me."

With my right hand, I kept the gun sighted on his ginormous center mass as I used my left hand to grab my shoulder mike to call a Code 99 into my radio. *Officer emergency!*

"You can't get away with this!" he taunted. Then he turned toward the water and started screaming, "Shoot me. Just shoot me! Go ahead! It's what you wanna do!"

Apparently, he was one of those people that talks with his hands, and as soon as he had them both in the air, I made my move. That's when Wharf, my 150-pound best friend and perpetual water baby determined this guy was going to jump and leapt to the rescue. You could call it premature eject-ulation. It was like dropping Little Boy and Fat Man in a tub—big plume—bigger fallout. From the top of my khaki marine patrol ball cap to my steel-toed boots, I was drenched.

"Help! Help! It's trying to kill me! Oh my God, I'm drowning! Help, somebody, help!" Down in the water I could see the big man thrashing around and Wharf struggling to get a grip on him to make the save.

My herd of sheep trailed onto the floating dock, causing it to sway like a Tilt-a-whirl. One old guy, who looked like Herbert Hoover on crack, handed me his glasses just as I realized he'd stripped down to his skivvies to assist with the rescue. I pushed him back into the rest of the flock and yelled at them, "Hang onto him!"

The alleged's—as we had been taught to say at the academy—woven bag was lying on the ocean bottom. I could see it because the water was only about four-feet deep.

"Stand up," I monotoned and then called a Code Four into the radio. "Everything's hunky-dory here. Forget that officer emergency thing."

"I can't swim! Help me! I'm drowning!" He flayed around as though he was reliving a scene from *Jaws*.

"STAND UP!" I yelled, and somewhat reluctantly—without looking away from the fray—slipped my Glock .45 back into its holster.

"Help me! I can't swim!" he kept screaming. In my experience in the Coast Guard in my last life, most drowning victims don't yell, and they never whine. He was in full-blown whine mode, but still bobbing around like beach ball in a boat wake.

"Oh for Pete's sake, just stand up and walk to the beach. Then get on your knees and put your hands behind your head."

Finally, my words seemed to enter the guy's giant cranium. He sloshed to shore, flinging bitter verbal insults the whole way, some of which I really had to question, since I don't think he's met my mother. Nonetheless, some were accurate. His contraband, the marshmallow bag, buoyed to the surface and floated behind him like a message tube from a submarine.

Wharf figured out there was no emergency by this point and doggy-paddled to shore all happy and awaiting his expected ration of hero worship. I was at a loss. Should I yell at him for pushing the guy in, or praise him for trying the rescue? Sometimes, I wanted to ditch him and work solo. This sheep dog didn't need a partner—didn't want a partner —had been my oft-repeated mantra. Now I had a best friend with fur.

Just push on, I said to myself. At least I had things under control again.

That's when I heard heavy breathing and footsteps thundering across the parking lot and onto the beach. Thunk! A longhaired dirt-bagger tackled us, knocking the wind out of me and a big toot out of the bad guy. As he and the shoplifter wrestled around on the sand, coating the shoplifter in a way that reminded me of my mother making fried chicken, I scuttled away on my hands and knees.

In my mind, I remembered learning in the academy that most law enforcement officer-involved shootings occur when the officer is in retreat mode, but I just couldn't see me winning the fight on the ground. Before I could call for assistance—again—the dirt-bagger had subdued my suspect.

Big eye roll. "Snake!" I muttered, as I grabbed the suspect and cuffed him.

"But Aloha…" he said.

"I can handle this myself." There was a lot of not-so-subtle eye-squinting and jaw-locking going on, which I'm sure the sheep were enjoying.

Yep, the dirt-bagger was my former husband—Eduardo Aquilae—and as I had recently learned, an undercover DEA agent. Most of his friends called him Eddie. I called him Snake—his biker name.

I have a modest tattoo on my ass as a reminder of our marriage that said, "Once bitten, twice shy." At this point, I'm not sure if he's a good man or not. The divorce was complicated, but so was our marriage. I guess they all are. Nonetheless, he treats me great—if by great, you mean remaining virtually non-existent for years at a time.

Apparently, he has no confidence in my cop skills. *Gee, I wonder why not?* I looked down at my uniform shirt. I had a big wad of gum stuck to the little Hawaiian Marine Patrol patch, my suspect was totally sand-basted and my partner was licking himself.

Even looking like a biker druggie, Snake exuded some kind of cocky confidence. He's what I like to think of as a real cop—a cop's cop. Me, I'm Baywatch with a gun. As a reserve marine patrol officer, the phrase "Seventy-one, a badge, and a gun" summarized my skills. I actually got ninety-one on the test, but that doesn't count for much in situations like this.

Snake had busted into my bust to save the day, of course, probably blowing whatever undercover scheme he had going.

"Aloha, you okay?" He looked scared. He never looks scared. I nodded. He slammed the fat man, who had struggled up to his knees, face down in the sand. Then he squeezed the cuffs tighter.

"Ow, that hurts!" You like to hurt people don't you?" Marshmallow Man sputtered out spit and sand. "The cuffs are too tight!"

"Don't worry. They'll stretch once you wear them awhile." Mr. Compassion had spoken. As a concession, I took a second set of cuffs and put one on the man's other hand, then hooked the two sets together and yoinked him to his feet.

"Dude, this is my call, I'll handle it," I said to Eddie, as I held the man with one hand and snapped on Wharf's leash with the other. The sheep had gone back to grazing. This was my wolf.

Snake raised his eyebrow, the one with a white streak through it, and dropped his hold on the big man's arm. He was looking a little wolf-like, but before we could fight, the sumo-sized suspect rudely interrupted us.

"My bag, my bag, I need my bag!" He demanded in a voice like Cartman from *South Park*.

I hoped he had a cover-up to match his ensemble, but a large beach towel would do the trick for me. Because of his size and the ensuing struggle, the T part of his swimsuit was merely a memory, showing too much cheek and no modesty—or dignity, for that matter.

"Watch him a sec' would you? I'll be right back." I sat down in the sand and freed my feet from my work boots, then peeled off my socks. I was tempted to squiggle my toes around in the hot sand for a minute, but I knew that would blow my last grain of credibility.

I waded into the water to retrieve the man's shoulder bag. I told Wharf to stay on the beach. He whined for a millisecond, then, as usual, followed his own agenda and stepped into the water far enough to fetch the marshmallow flotsam. I grabbed the bag from his soft grasp as I sloshed by him on my way back to dry land and stuffed it into the suspect's mesh carryall that was leaking water like a busted pipe.

It pissed me off that Wharf was willing to eat the evidence, but it didn't surprise me. It seemed like the pooch had an eating disorder and had been putting on weight. He'd already ransacked my lunch today, scarfing down my tuna sandwich and Nilla wafers, leaving me the apple that traveled to work with me on a daily basis until it was so brown I chucked it in my compost pile. I only bought about four apples a month, but hey, I had good intentions.

When I got back to Snake and the suspect, I muttered, "Fat, yellow, and useless. I should have shot him." It was all smack talk. Wharf's response was to shake a spray of water, give me a big sloppy kiss on the hand, and then complete his contrite trifecta with a whiz on a rock at the head of the dock.

"What's wrong? Nothing in there but an apple?" Snake seemed to be laughing at me. His lunch was the antithesis of mine. He took a new apple every day and then actually ate it.

He then slapped me on the ass and jogged away.

Funny thing about sheep and wolves, they hear what they want to hear. By the time I'd passed the shoplifter off for transport to jail and gone back to the main dock where my patrol boat was located, I had a message on my phone to call my supervisor.

"Hey, this is Aloha. What's up?" I asked my boss, Babs McKee. They call her "By-the-book-Babs." Her picture is in the dictionary next to the definition of anal-retentive. If she has a sense of humor, I figure she keeps it under lock and key, since I hadn't seen it yet. Still, I couldn't have imagined her response.

"You and your partner need to get your butts into the office—*wiki-wiki!*" *Wikiwiki* is the Hawaiian version of the word *pronto*. Like that was going to make me hurry.

"You're on administrative leave pending an investigation of your actions today." Then the phone went silent. I stared at it. It stared back. It showed a strong signal, plenty of power, yet no connection.

My guts responded with what felt like the need to pee or puke or both. I felt like I did as a kid when preparing for a spanking that I didn't deserve, mostly because of that little witch Mallory Kila. Did I say witch? I think you know what I meant to say.

Another of my basic truths in life is that people don't change. Kids that cut in line in kindergarten will cut you off in traffic when they're fifty. My theory—and a good one, I might add—doesn't relate so much to what-you-play-is-what-you'll-do, like mud pie maker to pastry baker, as much as you are who you are. I think we're all hard-wired from conception. As I mentioned, I'm a sheep dog. I watch things, I protect things and I try to fix things. Those are my strengths.

My weaknesses are many: I'm a hypochondriac, partially deaf, break more things than I fix, seem to have some strange black cloud over my head regarding men, and I have no mommy genes. The list goes on and on, but the worst is that I'm a pleaser.

Mallory Kila, my long ago nemesis, was the opposite. She was a wolf in little girl's clothing. She lied, she cried, she exploited weakness in others. Like all wolves, she excelled at ditching the lesser sheep dogs. In the vein of most predators, she was simply better at outwitting the prey than the sheep were at defending themselves. Then, as the ultimate insult, she'd blame the sheepdog's slow response for the carnage.

Because of her actions toward me, I used to get that same pee-or-puke feeling often when I was a kid. I didn't like it. And I didn't like thinking about Mallory, someone I'd long put behind me. Besides, I still had to figure out what I'd done wrong today.

Another thing: Sheepdogs don't run from trouble, they confront it. I jogged to my boat and commanded Wharf to hop onboard. I'd like to think it was obedience—but I know it was just because it was what he wanted to do—he obliged and I slammed my 25' aluminum patrol boat into gear.

Together we skimmed along West Maui's glassy coastline, me at the helm, Wharf riding shotgun, with the wind blow-drying his yellow coat. I got over my fit of hostility toward him as he hung his head over the side, trying to catch water spraying up from the gunwale.

His relentless optimism was contagious. I reasoned that Babs was just joking, if for no other reason than because she was overdue. This was not by the book, but maybe it was her idea of funny.

My anxiety dispelled as I sucked in the warm summer air. What looked like thunderclouds billowed above the West Maui Mountains. We hadn't had rain in weeks, nor was there any in the forecast. This left the water clearer than normal. Still, there was a hazy pall to the air as the volcano debris known as vog continued to blow in from the Big Island of Hawai'i.

A fish leapt off my starboard bow and for a moment, I longed for a light duty fishing rod and a free hour. Just the thought of catching a fresh *mahimahi* made my mouth water. Unfortunately, I felt By-the-Book's stopwatch ticking over my head, so I motored on at full speed.

Within an hour, I reached Ma'alaea Harbor near the center of the Valley Isle and tied the state's Hewes Craft to the dock. As I backed my truck to the boat ramp, an oppressive heat replaced the warm breeze I'd experienced while on the water. A glance in my truck's rearview mirror revealed worry lines on my suntanned face, crowned with a bad case of hat hair.

I had Brother Iz playing on the stereo in the truck singing about a place over the rainbow. I'd learned to love Hawaiian music since I'd moved back to the Islands. Part of the therapy for my previous hearing loss had been to reacquire my lost balance by learning to dance hula. My ears were still healing and now allowed me to access a few sounds, if not full speech, in that ear. I'd even gotten to where I could dive if I took out my hearing aid. I was discovering my new normal.

Wharf, as usual, had scampered up the ramp, recycled some of the ocean water onto the nearest tire, and impatiently waited for me to load him into the truck.

When we first started working together after I adopted him a year earlier, he would wait in the boat and bark directions while I backed the trailer into the water. I couldn't stand that kind of pressure, nor the public's comments on his cuteness. I tried threatening him, coaxing him, and dragging him, but I found bribery worked best.

Let's just say if powdered donuts ruled the world, Wharf would be their slave. My mom, Eve, had taught me to use the tools God gave me. Okay, so I have a weakness for powdered donuts too. I keep them in the truck to elicit Wharf's obedience. At least that's how I rationalize it.

Once I had the boat secured on the trailer, I checked the rigs nearby for expired license tabs. That daily chore done, we cruised out of the boat launch parking lot and made our way to the Kahului office.

Getting off work early, rediscovering my partner's best attributes, getting a glimpse of my scary, sexy ex-husband, and driving the boat too fast—life didn't get much better than that. I laughed at Babs's prank even before I got to her office. Whom did she think she was kidding?

A half hour later, I walked into her glass cubicle sporting a grin and a diet Coke. Wharf tagged along off-leash.

"What took you so long?" Babs barked at us. I looked at Wharf. He wasn't talking, so I answered for both of us.

"I refueled the boat, hosed it down, and unhooked the trailer," I said. "Oh, and I bought a soda. Did you want one?" I was quickly becoming just a tad less confident that Babs was in a joking mood.

"Aloha, sit down." Yikes! She usually called me Jones. Calling me Aloha was akin to calling me Snookum. Uh-oh… Maybe I should have hurried.

She waved me to one of two chairs backed up against a window that looked out into the main office. Wharf did a little hoppity-thing and landed in the other chair. Somehow, he curled his heavy-duty load of flesh and fur into the seat, but it didn't look comfortable. I did the same with similar results.

"Aloha," she said, as my inner child screamed "Yikes!" and danced in place as though she had to tinkle. "It seems like you were busy this afternoon. Why don't you tell me about it?"

Babs didn't blink, but she did run her hand through her short-cropped hair. I couldn't help but notice the scars from her most recent surgery to remove precancerous skin lesions. It was less a badge of survival than the grim reality of a lifetime's work under the sun on boats and beaches.

My inner voice—the hypochondriac—suggested I had better get myself checked for skin cancer. Another one said that at that moment, my job worries were the immediate threat. It was just my luck to have multiple inner personalities. My rational inner voice told the others to shut up. Instead, they milled around, scratching and muttering. They knew official questioning when they heard it.

I listed the contacts I'd made. "I stopped twelve boats today and did safety checks on all of them. I wrote one ticket for no water-ski observer and one for an eight year-old without a life jacket. We took a relief break at the quick mart at Mala Wharf and I caught a shoplifter. I checked the Ma'alaea Harbor parking lot for expired tabs. We came in when you called."

"What did you say to the shoplifter?" Babs had been flipping a pen around like a tiny baton. She now put the pen to paper.

I gave her the *Reader's Digest* version. I didn't mention that I had been at the market because Wharf had snagged my lunch, nor did I mention Wharf falling on the dock. There was no point in making my partner look bad, especially since he had his head draped over the armrest of his chair onto my leg.

He had that dreamy look in his eyes while he watched me talk. It's not that I'm so good to him. It is just that he sees the best in people and loves to be with me in particular. I stroked his silky occipital ridge and got all smushy inside. I was really regretting my earlier annoyance with him.

Maybe I needed to mellow out a little. I'd heard all the stats about cop stress: Sixty-seven percent divorce rate nationwide (ninety-nine percent for women), more likely to die by their own hand than another's, life span after retirement seventeen years less than a civilian of the same age.

This all ran through my head in the time it took me to take a deep breath. Ah, much better. I took a slug of my caffeinated nirvana.

Then Babs asked, "And at what point did you say—and I quote—'Fat, yellow, and useless; I should have shot him'?"

Diet Coke blew out my nose—Babs was going to need a new piece of paper.

Chapter Two

It seems that "innocent until proven guilty" applies to everyone but law enforcement personnel. Almost every jerk you see on the receiving end of the latest cop-gone-crazy-video did something to warrant the stop, if not the beating. The good news? I was not on administrative leave because of beating the guy. This official 'spanking' was for racial profiling. Since we were commissioned as a team, Wharf was now county property. He too had been relieved of duty. We were again in the same boat. This time, unfortunately, it involved a certain creek and no paddle.

I heard the *Cops* theme song in my head. What was I gonna do?

The accusation stung. I'm not a racist. And Wharf, he's a dog. He licks himself in public. He steals lunches. He slathers up the windows and he snores. He's an equal opportunity offender in regards to all the aforementioned habits. He's not a racist, either.

Despite my response to Bab's last question—that I'd been talking about Wharf, not the suspect—the political climate on Maui was such that I couldn't come back to work without a full inquiry.

Hours later, the *Cops* theme song about bad boys again played in my head. At almost nine o'clock on a Saturday night, I had watched the sun's final act as it set on my bedroom wall. Long rays of light—triangular and golden—made the surface glisten.

You see, I'm not really a full-time cop. I'm the Lahaina Harbormaster, but to make ends meet on Maui, I'd taken a part-time gig as a reserve marine patrol officer. A true weekend was a rarity. Nonetheless, I was in my new home, in bed, wide-awake and not alone.

By its very nature, my little hovel should have made me feel cozy. To say it was small was an understatement. However, involuntarily crunched into the smallest mass, my entire body screamed for freedom. I'd been watching television when the two alpha males in my bed had fallen asleep, leaving me to my own thoughts. Each had expanded like a wet sea monkey and together occupied the majority of the mattress. In my attempt to unfurl from my cramped position, I launched myself onto the tile floor with a thump.

Eddie opened his eyes and said, "Might want to try that with padding next time." Then he rolled onto his side. Wharf didn't even deign an acknowledgement.

You see, I needed to get a statement from Eddie about the accusation and well, one thing lead to another, and well, what can I say? There were a couple reasons besides the pleasant prospect of gorging myself on wedding cake that prompted me to marry him. I blushed at the thought.

Standing barefoot in the late evening light, I saw Wharf's paw reach up to seek a soft caress. I rubbed his tummy and he flopped over with his leg reaching out to me. As though he knew my thoughts, Wharf kept his paw on me in comfort. I knelt next to him and kissed the velvet stubble on his forehead while inhaling the scent of his fur. When I had no one last year after my sister Leibe moved back to the mainland, Nature busied herself filling the void by offering me Wharf. I had gratefully accepted the gift.

I stood and looked longingly at the big king-sized bed—one of my few luxuries. Rather than fight for space, I sought solace in my second indulgence, a hot tub nestled where the fence wrapped around the deck outside my bedroom. I stepped out of my special in-case-I-get-a-hot-date blue satin chemise, let it drop on the weatherworn wood, and placed my hearing aid on the chair. Then I lifted the top off the hot tub. As stepped into my favorite environment—water—I felt its soothing neutrality buoy my body and spirits.

There, I pondered my situation. The marine patrol job was a score, a serendipitous offshoot from being the Lahaina Harbormaster. It was a good part-time job and I needed it. For the first time in my life, I had a mortgage.

I didn't know if the racial profiling accusation would go public. I wasn't sure if I could stay in this community wearing the racist label, no matter the investigation's conclusion. What would happen if I couldn't stay? If I decided to leave, where would I go?

I took several deep breaths and submerged in the chlorinated froth. Then I held my breath. This was the one unbreakable rule of scuba diving. Never hold your breath. It's something I did all the time above and below water since I was a kid, just to see how long I could last.

One thousand one, one thousand two, one thousand three…

I felt the carbon dioxide build. This was suffocation, not drowning. I knew a lot about drowning. Unlike my Coast Guard experience where I did numerous body recoveries, my tenure on water rescue teams was more about salvation.

One thousand fifty-six, one thousand fifty-seven… While I held my breath, I debated: Was drowning or suffocation the metaphor for my current situation? I blamed my dearth of answers on oxygen deprivation. I kept pondering and counting.

At one thousand one hundred and twenty—an easy two minutes—I exhaled. If I'd been underwater at depth, I could have gone another minute, as long as I stayed at the same depth. Holding your breath while ascending was a sure recipe for an air embolism.

As my head emerged from the water, my good ear registered the hum of a small jet flying low overhead on approach to Kapalua's West Maui Airport. Even if the passengers could see me in the hot tub, I didn't worry about skinny-dipping. More people have seen me naked than I can recall. Besides, skinny-dipping would be a misnomer for sure. In the *T* and *A* departments, I am short on *T* and a little long on *A*.

I shifted my eyes from the jet to watching a rare bird swoop above the ridge, riding thermals in the sky as the sunset's last streaks slipped into the ocean. The bird's cries in the night—eerie to most—spoke to my soul. I have an unabashed love of Nature.

I shivered and looked at the thermometer. The water temperature had dropped from 102 to 98 degrees. Never one to seek room temperature, I rose from the tub, pushed the cover into place, and padded to the edge of the deck. With no railing, that particular safety feature—unfinished or broken like so many aspects of my home—was missing. I trembled. If I fell, I wondered if I'd bounce like a cartoon Road Runner or just hit with a splat like a ruptured bag of Acme cement. At twenty-feet above the grade, I figured either choice was bad.

My skin glistened in the last light of the photographer's golden hour as I felt the goose bumps rise on my flesh while I breathed in the evening air. Perhaps with my mind, body, and lungs refreshed, I could capture sleep.

I decided to grab a shower before reentering the competition for a spot in my bed. Under the spray, I sang the *Cops* theme song. Above the sound of my tone-deaf rap, the pulsating water, and a fan suitable for a toxic waste site, I thought I heard my phone ring, the original Star Trek theme my current ringtone. I skated barefoot across the tile and picked it up on the fourth ring.

"Aloha?" Sarang, one of my five sisters, spoke in a low, slow whisper.

"Hey Sis, *Aloha ahiahi.*" My greeting to her pretty well used up my Hawaiian vocabulary. Sarang had adopted the Hawaiian culture as her own since we were children, always shuttling back to the islands when on leave from the Marines.

Now that we were both out of the military, she had returned to a little cabin our family had near Hana. Her retirement surprised me, but I sensed it had been prompted by a passion for the Islands. In contrast, my return was prompted by an underwater explosives accident, a passion for watersports, and the fact that there are virtually no snakes in Hawai'i—the one in my bed being a notable exception.

Sarang, on the other hand, had immersed herself in the Hawaiian way, especially, since she had moved back to Maui. She still tried to enchant me whenever she could. Despite her mostly blonde hair, she said she felt the native drums beat in her veins.

She lives in a remote valley known for *taro* and a decent beach break. I hadn't been to that incestuous community in years and it would take an act of God to get me back. I had enough problems without sticking my toe into the murky waters of my past that to me, still swirled near Hana.

Sarang must have heard my mental challenge. "I need you to come here." Before I could stammer an excuse, she said, "There's a fire."

"What do you mean?" I asked.

"The forest," she said. "The forest's on fire."

"Then pack your stuff and leave." It seemed simple enough to me. I mean, really, she's a retired Marine. Granted I hadn't been to see her since she had moved back full-time as I had an issue with Hana, but she hadn't been to see me either. This would be a perfect opportunity for her to come to Lahaina and we could catch up.

"I can't," she said. "I can't leave."

"Why not?"

"Aloha, please, just come. Tonight. Now. Please." Her voice became quieter as she spoke. "I can't leave."

It sounded like an act of God to me. I looked back at my bed where Wharf and Snake snored in unison. It might be a good time to go after all. I could justify walking away from this pack by being a sheep dog and running to my sister's rescue.

Chapter Three

"She said there's a brush fire and that everyone has to evacuate," I explained to Eddie while Wharf eavesdropped. Brush fires in Hawai'i were becoming increasingly more common as sugarcane and pineapple fields had been left fallow, with water redistributed to people and away from agriculture.

Even though Sarang lived on the eastern—and thus wetter—side of the island, from what she said, this particular fire looked like it was jumping from ridge to ridge fueled by strong trade winds and dense, dry foliage caused by what could only be called a drought for that area.

Snake absorbed the information that I was heading toward historic Hana with a cop's calm while I crammed my clothes into a heavy nylon duffle bag. Although we had been married a short time, a long time ago, he knew why I'd made it a policy never to go back there.

Born in Hawai'i, I had grown up around the world but had returned to attend my first two years of college on Maui. I made the choice to be a little away from Oahu where my dad had been stationed but not a huge jump from home, like the mainland. In hindsight, I should have gone farther. That time in my life represented many things, few of them good.

I sighed as I packed. Snake kept his eyes closed and said, "You needed to go back sometime, may as well be now."

He needed to work on his empathy skills.

"You don't know what it's like," I replied.

He didn't rise to the bait. Instead, he said, "Time to get over it, Aloha."

I hate that voice—calm, quiet, reasonable—I should have known he would never really be in a motorcycle gang. He was a sheepdog at heart, just one with mad camouflage skills, more like a chameleon than a gecko.

Still, I didn't reply. I knew he'd never understand my fear of ostracism. He was a guy that fit in wherever he landed. Especially on Maui. His half-Hispanic and half-white heritage that produced dark skin and dishwater blonde hair allowed him to blend in with the locals.

While I'd studied isolation as a child, moving from base to base with my crazy family, I had my final exam in college, where I'd met Eddie in a whirlwind romance cloaked in a rebound. My jumpstart relationship with him hadn't caused my downfall, though it had its share of grief. I became a pariah by being in the wrong place when Brother Love died.

To the Hawaiians, Brother symbolized success. As an artist, he had earned international recognition and acclaim for his work in wood, likened to Chihuly's work in glass. At the time, he had attained fame, if not fortune, holding a coveted tenured position at the University of Hawai'i on Maui. An educated man, he was handsome, talented, and charismatic—the perfect professor.

In addition to his passion for art, he served as one of several local *kahunas*. By Brother's accounting, he was not so much a theologian, but more of a counselor and spiritual technician. When he died, anger eclipsed the locals' grief. And… their anger needed a target.

"They still blame me for Brother's death," I said, as I pulled on my favorite cargo shorts and Roxy T-shirt. I mentally dropkicked myself for using a semi-whiny voice similar to the one used by my earlier arrestee.

"No they don't, Aloha. That's history. No one cares about history anymore." Snake rolled onto his side and rubbed his eyes. He got a whiff of the hand he'd used to rub Wharf's belly and shuffled, buck-naked, to the bathroom sink to wash.

I watched covertly while I pretended to pack. To say it was good to see him was an understatement.

"In the Islands, history is everything," I said, as I gathered my basic needs for up to a week at Sarang's, plus everything I could imagine that I might possibly use to help her save the cabin. I should have been a Boy Scout.

"From creation, to the explorers, to the wars, to Brother Love's death, to today's arrest; it's all about history. I can show you the photo. Everyone remembers the photo. I made the tabloids for crying out loud."

My voice took on an accusing tone. I paused to think about taking the path toward a tiff with my ex-husband. This was not his fault. At twenty-two, I had been young and stupid—never naive.

Even though years had passed since I had fully realized the power of photography, the resultant feelings were etched in stone. Back then I had been supplementing a few scholarships with my job in the art department—my secret job.

I had since learned that secrets are the most common sign of stress in the mentally ill. This particular secret caused much the same result over the years. I had been the nude model in Brother's figure drawing classes. That morsel of tasty gossip became public via the last person I expected to violate my privacy—the person who had hired me—Brother Love. Brother knew my family. He promised that none of them would know I stripped naked for money.

When he died, Brother's death exposed more than my skin.

In his students' drawings, my flesh was little more than a widely interpreted still life representation of humanity. Some added weight to their drawings. For others, my soul inhabited a stick figure. Rarely did anyone unveil the shyness hidden in my eyes. Somehow, Brother had captured that emotion in his carvings.

Snake too, had a gift for reading my eyes. He had often attempted to diffuse my angst with humor and love, not always well-suited allies. On his return to bed, he wrapped his arms around my waist as he blew hot breath on the back of my neck. "Time for a quickie before you go?"

Umm... I felt a weakening. I challenged the feeling by engaging him. "You're not listening to me." I pulled away.

"Take your clothes off and I'll listen to you." This was his standard answer to the whole left-brain, right brain, men-learn-differently-than-women discussion.

"Errr..." I growled and feigned to push him away.

In response, he said, "But I like that picture of you. You looked so innocent." He pulled me back into his arms and rubbed against me.

"Looks can be deceiving." I let him keep rubbing.

Looks were a major issue, then and now. One shouldn't equate nude modeling with tremendous beauty or soft-focused porn. To be the perfect art-school model, all you need is the willingness to hold still several hours a day and not shave your underarms. I wasn't perfect. Shaving is a must. The job paid for tuition and a couple surfboards. Despite the stigma, I favored the work.

At twenty-two, I had modeled for Brother's classes, clung to my shyness, and made a few bucks while I learned the finer points of art. Even though I knew I'd need to enter a branch of the military soon, art was simply my rebellion. Brother had been working on a one-man show for a gallery in Honolulu. Consumed with creating human totems that morphed into shapes of nature, I was his favorite model. My facial structure, with my slight Native American heritage, hinted at the look of a classic Hawaiian with subtle Teutonic highlights. The wood didn't know my hair and eyes were the wrong color.

During May of my senior year, with the graduation art show looming, Brother would meet me in his studio where he would methodically hew a Koa log into "The Fish Woman."

It was a win-win proposition for everyone except Nate Deems, my boyfriend at the time. If clues were shoes, he would've been barefoot. He didn't know about my job.

Snake interrupted my musings by running his hands down my back. Something seemed to be pushing us apart. Guess it was the rubbing. Never a quitter, he grabbed my ass and again began kissing my neck, pausing long enough to say, "Too bad, Brother was guilty..." Snake was willing to open the wound and clean it. Ask anyone. They'll tell you the process is painful, although it lessens the scarring.

This time I pulled away and picked up my swimsuit. "Brother was dedicated to his culture, his art and his students." I recited the party line.

"Aloha, I checked the file. He overdosed. He didn't have an orgiastic heart attack."

"That's not true." I stopped packing with a wife beater tank top folded in my hands. I had assumed that the stress of production, tenure, and an illicit affair had killed him. I'd made it my fault and so had everyone else. I didn't know the half of it.

"Suit yourself." Snake said, as he crawled back into bed. "That's what the coroner's report said." He sat in bed with his back against the wall and his fingers laced behind his head. He didn't look like a DEA agent or a dirt-bagger. He looked like someone I wanted to crawl back into bed with, but instead, I decided to take the fight.

"I thought we didn't keep secrets, Snake." This was an old rule in our relationship. Obviously, one we had both ignored or we wouldn't be divorced.

"There's a difference between secrecy and privacy Aloha. It was confidential. Now you need to know. Don't make a big thing out of it." Again, he gave me the cop lecturing voice. I *really* hate that voice.

"Why tell me now?"

"It didn't come up until now. Plus, you're finally going back to Hana. You need to know the truth, not what everyone wants to believe. Brother was no saint."

It had all happened on Mom's Weekend. At the time, my dad, Ike, had been deployed out of the country with my mom, Eve, at his side, so I hadn't worried about participating in the various activities and festivities. I just stuck with my regular work schedule.

However, when Mallory Kila's mother showed up at Brother's office—for I-don't-know-what-reason—she found me naked and asleep. Unfortunately, my repose was on the floor next to the partially nude body of Brother Love. Partially nude meant no shirt and… his sleep was permanent. Completing the scene was a collection of the *kahuna's* traditional objects: masks, rattles, costumes, charms and boxes. These accoutrements, described as sex toys in the tabloids, completed the package.

Once Mallory's mom, Betty Kila, got over her shock, something that must have taken milliseconds—she captured a series of photos before calling for help. Let's just say Mallory—that little wolf I remembered from my childhood holidays in Hana—was definitely her mother's daughter.

The staff, students and administrators working in the building witnessed my awakening. Mallory's mother handed the images to her daughter's best friend Dee Dee Nagasako, an ambitious journalism major. The story and photos were printed locally, and then had been picked up by the Associated Press—as had budding journalist Dee Dee Nagasako.

In the era of political correctness, the idea of a white model for native art provided the right level of sensationalism alongside the body of a dead kahuna. The story sold better than fireworks during Chinese New Year. The nudity and so-called sex toys were definite bonuses.

Within twenty-four hours, the university had unceremoniously graduated me with a degree in Fine Arts and I joined the Coast Guard. This suited my father's plan, as all six of us girls were expected to join the military.

Within days, it seemed that had I clicked my heels together three times and learned that Dorothy was right. Not only was there was no place like home, I officially had no home.

Along the way, I'd married Eddie, divorced Eddie, and gotten a tattoo to punctuate both life-changing events. Since then, I'd had a series of temporary abodes and extended travels, feeding my desire for deliberate impermanence, even to the extent that I lived on boats whenever possible. This new life on Maui was an experiment in normalcy.

Now, late on this August evening, I prepared to face that painful part of my past all over again. Sarang was more than a sister—among my five all-female siblings—she was nearest in age to me. We'd spent some amazing weekends at the cabin in that little valley on the way to Hana, with and without the rest of the family. She understood me well. I knew she wouldn't ask me to return on a whim.

Sarang's name, like all of ours, was the word for "love" in the different geographical locations each of us was born. Our Dad chose our middle names for the Air Base at which he was stationed at the time of our births. Hence, my name is Aloha Hickam Jones. My oldest sister is Leibe Ramstein Jones to immortalize the family's time in Germany. Sister number two is Amoré Aviano Jones with a nod to Italy. Sarang's middle name is Osan, as she had been born in Korea. My next youngest sister's name is Love Lakenheath, commemorating our time in England. Our baby sister's name is Viva Nellis, a result of my dad's assignment in Nevada. I guess my parents couldn't find a word for "love" in Vegas-ese.

Snake interrupted my reverie with a shocker when he said, "Tell her I said 'Hi.'" Then he added, "And I love her."

"Jeez, Eddie, she's not sick." I didn't see his face flush as I pushed a Big Dog nightgown on top of everything else in my bag and yanked the zipper shut. "Why tell her that? It'll only make her nervous—or mad."

You don't want to make a Marine mad, even a recently retired Marine. When we had been married, Snake and Sarang hadn't been close. I don't know why, but I wasn't telling anyone in the family I was seeing him again… if that's what you'd called this evening's interlude.

"She's lot like you," he said, with his eyes closed and his hand on Wharf's belly.

It made me swallow hard. Maui was my first real home in years. Minutes ago, I had tried to figure out how to leave. Now I wanted to stay. Then he said, "Take your dive gear." I knew he meant my wetsuit and snorkel set. My favorite surfing and diving had been off that remote coast. I didn't see any reason to pack these for a wildfire and said as much.

"You never know and it won't take much space."

True that. Besides, I kept my gear bag in Buffy's trunk for just such opportunities. Buffy is my name for Snake's Mustang that my parents had purchased from him and gifted to me when I moved back to the Islands. As I packed, I opened the small gun locker embedded in the back wall of the closet, another of the former owner's important sales-appeal details, where I grabbed my Glock and stuffed it into a pancake holster on my waist. I stowed my locking gun case in in the trunk.

"I can tell this is going to be a disaster," I said, slogging down the hall with my soft canvas bag of clothes over my shoulder. "I'm never leaving home again." My eyes got all gooey.

"It'll be okay, Eeyore," my darling ex-husband taunted from my bed. "You taking the boy?"

I gave him the "duh" look as Wharf trotted down the hall after me with his leash in his mouth.

Chapter Four

Within ten minutes, Snake was out the door and I was on the road with my best friend, Wharf, asleep in the back seat of my island cruiser. The primer black muscle car was badass.

As I accelerated down the hill toward the Honoapi'ilani Highway, my Diet Coke tipped over and glugged onto the carpet. "There's no freaking cup holder in this thing," I complained aloud to Wharf. I'm always a hostile driver without a caffeine fix. Not a night person, nor, for that matter, a morning person, the soda was my energizer. Hell on wheels at midday, by two-thirty, I usually need a nap. It was going to be a long night.

The drive to Hana with its 600 hairpin turns had begun. It never ceased to amaze me that convicts with pickaxes carved this narrow path in 1926. Anymore there was never a perfect time to travel this famous route, but at least in the late evening there shouldn't be much traffic.

Wharf had no response to my cup holder complaint. The pooch—big, yellow, and built like a *Los Angeles*-class submarine—sprawled across the backseat, all four legs splayed in the air. It was one of his many funny habits. When he wanted attention, he would slap his big scratchy paw on me. In greeting, he willingly exchanged bodily fluids by using his cold wet nose and a warm sloppy tongue. I guess it works well for him, since I usually shrieked, gagged, and giggled in response.

You know… Wharf and Eddie have a lot in common.

At the bottom of the hill, I drove south toward the Pali. The thunderclouds I had seen earlier over the West Maui Mountains blended with a gloomy haze of volcanic fog ghosting in from the Big Island. Alongside the road, the twilight revealed crew-cut sugar cane fields converted to desert wasteland where giant rusty machinery had once lumbered along like dinosaurs.

I only slowed from Mach 4 to the legal speed as I passed through Olawalu, Ma'alaea and Waikapū on my way to Kahului to bisect the island and gas up the beast.

Between the last two towns, I pulled over for Wharf to water a mile marker. He practiced passive resistance. I scowled at him. He yawned in response, then sat, and repeatedly licked his leg fur down to his toes. He was pouting because I hadn't stopped to let him swim at either Olowalu or Ma'alaea. The smell of wet dog in a warm car is not one of my favorites. Wharf lives for water. He sees himself as the pearl in the world's calciferous shell. I wondered how this attitude would wear at Sarang's as my patience plummeted. Finally, he went over and claimed the mile marker for Planet Dog then kicked some dirt around to make a point.

When we climbed back in the car, it smelled like dry dog. I could breathe this smell for a lifetime. Thank God, Snake isn't the jealous type, not that it matters. Tonight's hook-up had been a one-time deal. Really.

As we drove, I observed the full effect of the mountains splitting Maui to create the Valley Isle. Not long ago it seemed like the eastern side was my past, and West Maui my future. As kids, our family had spent holidays near Hana camping at Wai'anapanapa and visiting Auntie Ruth.

After Sarang and her husband Frank joined the Marines, they had made the cabin their home base. Until my downfall, it was a place of romping childhood memories in a community perhaps more foreign than many of the places my dad had been stationed overseas, since we had always lived on base.

Tonight, I couldn't help but reflect on my place here at all. Had I ever truly belonged? Did I care anymore? My history still nipped at my psyche, as did my recent accusation. Snake and the Eagles were probably right: "Get over it."

"My mind is wandering more than your nose." I cleaned up my language for Wharf's sake even though he probably couldn't hear me as he had his head shoved out the window with his floppy ears flying and his lips fluttering in the wind.

I noticed that the closer we moved to our destination, the greater the haze. It was a metaphor of my life. Wharf and I made our passage across the island, if not comfortably back in time, at least in relative harmony. I thought about Eddie and the wisdom of my recent choice. I had loved him once, I don't know if I ever stopped. I shook off the reverie and tuned in the radio.

As we passed through Pa'ia—another relic from the sugarcane days—I heard more information about the wildfire on the radio. The poor air quality was more than just a bad case of fog. "Holy Crappoly! The smoke is already getting thick!" This time I could see by Wharf's look that he didn't appreciate my tone.

As darkness enveloped our journey, the trade winds calmed. At Ho'okipa, this late in the day, there were no cars parked at one of the world's most famous windsurfing sites.

After that we dropped down into Māliko Bay, I remembered the rodeos we'd attended at the little arena there with Maui's most famous *paniolos* competing for cash and prizes. The unlikely combination of rodeo and tropical islands was one of the biggest anomalies of Hawai'i. These islands once were also home to giant cattle companies. Agriculture of all kinds had been the foundation of island life.

Hawaiians believed *taro* was the creator of life and man, the cultivator of *taro*. It was a circle and cycle of renewal. *Taro* corms—pineapple-sized tubers grown in water-filled fields, or *lo'i*—were pounded into the Hawaiian starch staple know as *poi*. *Taro*, and subsequently *poi*, are to Hawaiians what potatoes are to Americans and rice to Asians. Hawai'i's best *taro* is grown near Hana in a community that has successfully clung to the past and effectively dodged the future.

Even with the smoke, I captured glimpses of the sea between tropical forest glades as we wove our way up through Ha'ikū. This is another idyllic community melded between the beach and the volcano just before you get to Jaws, one of the most famous big wave surf spots in the world. It was on my list to visit, though not to surf, as it's beyond my skillset by light years. Since it is also on the infamous Hana Highway, I'd managed to procrastinate visiting it for over a year since moving back to Maui.

The miles passed slowly, each bend taking us into greater darkness as we waited our turn to cross one-lane bridges. There was virtually no traffic heading to Hana but a veritable exodus coming from the opposite direction. At Ke'anae, a sign notified us the road to Hana was closed to all except local traffic.

"Hey, are you happy to finally visit Hana?" I asked Wharf, who had just crawled into the front seat where he sat in regal repose. We rounded another turn as I was scratching the place behind his silky ear that makes him go argh-argh-argh. Instead, I heard a low rumble in his throat. "Aarrghhh!" I screamed, and slammed on the brakes at a makeshift roadblock, stopping just short of taking a local law officer off his feet.

With a timid smile and an apology, I attempted to make nice as I rolled down the nearly vintage window. Officer Haspin—according to his nametag—had sweat stains under his arms and a pre-cardiac glow to his complexion. He started it with me when he said with a Pidgin accent, "Restricted area. You gonna hafta turn around."

The sign read "Local Traffic Only" so I said, "I'm local."

"Listen, Missy, dis here da road to da fire. You no go dere."

My attitude switched from contrite to contrary.

"I was born here. Were you?"

Haspin hiked up his polyester blues and said, "This is restricted access. Got to be Hawaiian to get to da fire, and Blondie, you ain't local."

Just then, another vehicle pulled up behind me. In my rearview mirror, I could see one of the Nooner brothers I remembered from my youth. I couldn't remember which one, since there were four of them close together in age and each named after one of the four main Hawaiian gods: Kū, Kāne, Lono and Kanaloa. Even as a kid I thought it was kind of ballsy to name kids after gods, especially since they'd all been of sketchy character. Auntie Ruth called them the Loony-Nooners. Involuntarily I ducked and hoped he wouldn't recognize me. I don't know why, since it had been years since I'd seen anyone from this community, but if I recognized him, I figured he might remember me too.

Rather than explain that I was coming to help my equally "not local" sister, I decided to use my law enforcement identification to get through the roadblock. As I dug around in my handbag to find it, Wharf leaned over to help. A long, warm stream of liquid love trickled down my neck as I grabbed my waterproof wallet. Shifting in the seat to wipe away the drool with one hand and hold my wallet with the other, I accidentally released the clutch. The Mustang jumped forward a few feet before it stalled. Haspin had his hand on his gun and his finger on the trigger by the time I looked up. It wasn't a good thing.

"Here's my ID," I said, as I held my wallet out the window. He moved his finger from the trigger to the indexed position. I appreciated the accommodation.

When he got a look at my ID his eyes widened, his brows raised, and a ready-to-whistle pucker formed on his lips. As he sucked in his breath, Nooner shouted from his red pickup truck, "Come on, Dog! Let's go!"

Haspin took his hand off his weapon, wrote the date on my windshield with an orange paint pen, and waved me through with one finger as he yelled, "Shaka Kū!" With a grin, he gave Nooner the wave through without a stop. At first, I attributed it to reverse discrimination. Kū looked Hawaiian, even though he's half Filipino. Then I noticed that his windshield already sported an orange date. I sheepishly put my paranoia away while my inner voices argued about closet space.

"Back for less than five minutes and I'm already pissed off." I gave Wharf a "talk to the paw" gesture in case he had a reply. He didn't.

The smoke thickened and to me it smelled good, like a giant campfire or the scent from the *Pirates of the Caribbean* ride at Disneyland. In reality, I knew it was neither of those and took a deep breath to get my focus, only to end up coughing up the acrid air.

Again, I turned up the radio and heard the local announcer say that wildfires blazed on both sides of Hana, each started in the lightning storm the previous afternoon. He also reported the placement of the 'alala, a relative of the crows, ravens and jays, on the endangered species list, thereby halting construction of a much needed road-widening. The final news bulletin announced a study stating that homicide is the leading cause of death in pregnant women in Hawai'i. Thirty-eight percent: How sick is that?

Without a second thought, I turned onto Hana Road where it wound along the river through a federally protected bamboo stand. Unfortunately, the fire didn't respect environmental law.

When I reached the bridge's center span, its lights increased the visibility. My peripheral vision caught movement upstream. There, with a corona of flames silhouetting them stood two Axis deer on an island midstream. Indigenous or not, it didn't matter. They were huddled together on a tiny sanctuary from the fire. The slope behind them an inferno. I could feel the heat from the blaze in the car. How would they survive?

While I watched from my perch, I saw the fire jump the river. Maybe it was only an ember, but the brush on the other side exploded. By now, I had my window down and I felt a burst of warm wind hit my face. The tallest tree on the bank erupted in flames until only the crown burned bright. The wind pushed the fire on its way, stopped by no one and nothing, not even the river. I pressed my foot to the floor and raced toward my sister's home.

As the road again rose, the pall closed in and soon I passed a vista pullout. This route usually offered a spectacular view of the valley with the river bisecting it. On the south side of the river was Hana town. In the old days, enemies had known it as profoundly insular and relentlessly private. It hadn't changed much.

I knew that if I couldn't see downriver that I wouldn't be able to see upriver to where the new hydroelectric dam ruled the valley. Built recently, the concrete monolith created a reservoir that placed some of the original road underwater, along with the remains of an old *heiau* or Hawaiian temple. From a diver's perspective, I thought that exploring these relics was better than not diving, yet not nearly as interesting as plunging into in the open ocean's intriguing depths.

From a local perspective, construction of the dam once threatened to vanquish their *raison d'être*—the *taro*. Without a constant clean flow of water, the *lo'i* would not produce the crop. Some accommodation had occurred, and now both coexisted.

My stomach clenched. I adjusted my concentration from the roads in my past to the one on which I now drove. Tonight, due to the darkness and smoke, I could only see a couple of car lengths in front of me. Other than the hazy orange glow marking the fires, there was no hint of open sky.

"Maui's had plenty of wildfires over the years, but nothing like this," I said, mostly to myself, since Wharf had again crawled into the back seat and sacked out.

The 'ukulele music on the radio stopped and the announcer delivered an update. He sounded exhausted, but determined to keep everyone up on the latest conditions. "…flames sighted about a quarter-mile off Hana Road. Firefighters are standing by those structures determined defensible. They face difficult decisions. This means abandoning some homes and outbuildings, the first considerations must be for the firefighters' safety and success. Now we're going live to the base camp at the church, where

Hana Police Chief Lon Dhong Jr. is holding a press conference."

Lon Dhong? His name sounded like he could be a porn star. And, he's a junior. What were his parent's thinking? I thought Aloha was a name you gave a kid you wanted teased at school. Lon Dhong would elicit merciless taunting.

"Chief Dhong, what's the status on the Hono'māele Ridge portion of the fire?"

"We have almost a hundred firefighters and ten rigs working that fire. We're due for a shift change tomorrow morning at oh-six hundred hours and we'll have more information at that time."

The man, reading from a script, gave no hint as to the inferno's true nature. He didn't sound like a porn star, but the concept had left a mental picture of him in my brain.

"Chief, are any residents trying to defend the buildings you have abandoned?"

As he began to answer, I turned off the radio, slowed the Mustang, and passed two hose trucks alongside the road. A few hundred feet ahead was my sister's home—with no fire trucks nearby. From the looks of things, it had been deemed indefensible, thus virtually selected to burn. My chest felt tight and I unconsciously clenched my teeth. Only by blanking out these emotions could I keep from crying.

Chapter Five

Just as it had been when I said goodbye years earlier, my sister's decrepit island cruiser languished in front of her medicinal garden. Still, something was missing.

When Sarang and her husband Frank had purchased the cabin from the family, the tiny old cane shack emerged from the edge of the forest like a forgotten birdhouse. I could see someone had been busy felling surrounding *koa* and *ōhi'a lehua*. Pre-inferno, these trees had given the cabin cool shade in the summer and a rain canopy in the winter. Without the vegetation up to the edge of the cabin, I could see the rust on the corrugated metal roof. My headlights flashed on the droplets of water pouring forth from the sprinklers onto the wooden structure. The glistening moisture highlighted the rust's ambivalence toward the tenacity of the metal.

I parked behind Sarang's car and invited Wharf to join me outside our ride. I stretched and inhaled the dark, smoke-filled air. Wharf did the same, and then quickly relieved himself on Sarang's hubcaps.

We approached the tongue-and-groove *koa* door and my heart did that flibbity-thing again—definitely some kind of arrhythmia. The door was propped open by a water jug, but the old screen inside was shut. Before I could decide whether to knock or walk in, I saw Sarang turn from her neatly organized roll top desk. The yellow glow of a rare incandescent bulb backlit her lanky form.

"Hey, I was wondering when you'd get here."

That was it, no scream of joy, no rushing into my arms, no sobbing. There was a wildfire burning over the next ridge, with nothing but fuel between it and her home, yet my sister remained calm. That serenity had served her well in the past, but it seemed even more entrenched now, which was at stark contrast to her phone call.

Then she said, "Who's that?"

I looked down where Wharf sat obediently next to me, waiting for an invitation into the house. "His name is Wharf."

Sarang sighed. When she turned away, I saw tears well in her eyes and edge onto her tanned cheek. She shook her head from side to side indicating that she couldn't speak.

What the heck? I'd never seen her cry. Not even when Frank died.

For no good reason I said, "Snake said to say hi." Sarang sighed again and waved me in. I left Wharf on the porch in misery. He has abandonment issues. I don't know why.

Inside the cabin, the air was cooler and held the slight scent of fresh cut herbs and oil-based paint. It smelled of nature, comfort, and home. Sarang had always dabbled in painting and herbal therapy. Her specialty was bold color in primitive designs depicting local native legends. Brother had been her first art teacher too. The circle, instead of being complete, had imploded later.

She jarred me when she said, "I love you and I've missed you, but we have a few things to do before this place is turned to charcoal. I've already moved the tipi to Māko's. Stinger is around here somewhere."

The tipi was missing! God only knows why Sarang and Frank had built it, but over the years, there hadn't been a natural, native, earth-influenced Hawaiian mysticism, she had missed. This seemed contrary to her having been a career Marine. She and Frank had lived in the tipi during their visits as they refurbished the cane house. Nonetheless, the tipi belonged at Māko's Mercantile—a junk store with a fancy name. Māko had been saying for years that his place would be a museum. Somewhere between the rusty cars and a 1970s harvest gold refrigerator filled with clothespins, the museum dream looked a lot like a dump. Until I moved away, I thought Māko's represented the epitome of an old tourist trap. The more I traveled, the more I learned. Other towns were far poorer. Either way, it was great that the tipi was now a part of Māko's Mercantile and Museum.

Then the second important fact hit me.

"Stinger's here? Oh my gosh! *Kaikua'ana*! I'd better get Wharf back in the car before all heck breaks loose!" In a flash, I reverted to my childhood name for Sarang. It was the Hawaiian word for older sister and one she hated.

I called Wharf. My monster partner was MIA.

"Wharf!" I hollered toward the ridge. "Here boy, come on, come to Mommy." I had suddenly referred to myself in the third person when talking to the dog—embarrassing, gross, and disgusting—but probably not my worst fault.

"There they are, Aloha. They're fine." Sarang pointed down the road to where Stinger had Wharf on the run, nipping his flanks as he dashed toward the house. The poor guy was trying to hold his tail under his belly and look back to avoid the next attack. That is how fifty pounds of black tongue and attitude downed my intrepid partner.

"Sarang, call Stinger off before she kills him!" I begged. Wharf is all love, no fight. Stinger is a gray-bearded Chow Chow, who doesn't know she's a little old dog. I'd heard from Ruth that she saw herself as the defender of all Sarang owned and lived in a constant state of paranoia. Her territory extends well beyond Sarang—the only person she considers worth defending. Sarang had found her hanging around the cabin when she moved back. I'd heard this had caused some neighborly tiffs. I guessed there'd been several curses murmured, and a few shots fired—the feisty Chow Chow's demise the goal. Sarang's healing ways compensated for

Stinger's unpopularity, and the old biddy continued to thrive at her advanced but indeterminate age.

Sarang called Stinger off Wharf's belly. He shook the attack off with his usual aplomb. Stinger, I could tell, wanted to have back at him.

I immediately switched gears. "What shall I do? Want me to pack your stuff? Do you know what you need? Did you already move your jars?" I knew that Sarang would get her medicinal herbs and paints to safety first.

"We're not moving anything. Period." Sarang muttered, as she walked away from me, a flashlight in hand.

I couldn't believe that my sister would let everything burn. My eyes, already inflamed from the smoke, welled with tears, either that or some kind of blinding disease in its early stages. *Dear Hypochondria, Now is not a good time.* As I swiped my hands over them, Sarang hustled off toward the springhouse where I could hear the pump plugging away.

"Sarang, what in the holy hell are you planning?" I raced after her, not realizing that approaching Sarang from the back was forbidden. In two steps, I heard the growl, and before the third, I felt Stinger's mouth on my calf. I was surprised to hear Wharf's deep growl in response. Nobody touches his mommy.

"Sarang, call off your damn dog!"

In a quiet, calm voice, Sarang said, "Stinger, drop! Aloha, watch your language." Sarang kept walking to the springhouse, and Stinger ran after her stubborn mistress. From the back, they were quite a pair—both appeared to wear loose fluffy skirts, sashaying from side-to-side at a quick, steady clip. Stinger's black fur pants laced with gray matched my sister's faded sari. Both favored a toes-out form, resulting in plenty of bounce with each step. Sarang's short ponytail matched Stinger's flag of a tail.

"Sarang Osan Jones, stop this minute!" A shout wasn't necessary. My tone spoke for itself. My sister turned with a flinch and then adopted a bland look.

I had used this tactic infrequently. The first time was when I was five and needed to know something about something. I don't remember what about what.

"You have to help me defend the house." By her sharp tone, I could tell my sister was at her wit's end.

Even though I had known this stubborn woman all my life, her statement stunned me. She wanted us to save a building from a tenacious force of nature, when those trained to do so had determined the venture unsafe. I knew Sarang wouldn't be asking—or rather demanding—unless she *had* to make this stand. Material possessions had never been important to her, so I didn't understand this turnaround.

"Can we set some ground rules, you know, some safety parameters?" My training as a public safety diver was showing. This statement gave Sarang the answer she wanted. I would fight this battle with her; but I still needed an escape plan.

Sarang exhaled deeply and said, "We'll take rotating shifts—one sleeps, and the other keeps the water running. If the fire begins to blow flames, we'll leave. I won't let Frank's cabin fall victim to a loose ember or a creeping brush fire." Aha, she had answered my silent question. This was about Frank. It surprised me. Although she had grieved deeply following his death, she had never memorialized him before.

Without another word, we checked the pump and the generator. I clamored up a ladder to the roof and Sarang handed me her lawn sprinklers. With board and batten wood siding, the walls were the greatest source of danger—that and the surrounding forest.

By this time, it was pitch black outside and we had every safety measure in place. Because I had spent the previous hours traveling, Sarang told me to sleep first, assuring me that we'd change shifts at sunrise. She left me in the cabin while she delivered sandwiches, cookies, and drinks to the firefighters down the road.

Wharf and Stinger had reached the kind of truce that is possible only when the less aggressive dog is one hundred-plus pounds heavier, and willing to sleep with one eye open. Wharf camped on the tapa-inspired rug next to the couch. His snores and sighs made me smile and think of Eddie.

For me, getting to sleep is like trying to grab the brass ring while perched on a manic merry-go-round. Tonight I was exhausted, and fell asleep despite my rushing adrenaline, only to be startled awake by a siren at three a.m.

For some reason, when I awoke, I knew the emergency vehicle wouldn't pass Sarang's. The noise, emanating from its mechanical screamer, raised goose bumps on my skin. The high-pitched screech caused Wharf to add his deepest, darkest howl to the night. Stinger added her sharp yips to his penetrating *basso profundo*. The vehicle, driven with its siren squealing and its emergency lights spattering the night sky, sped up the dark dusty driveway and didn't quiet the air until stopping abruptly in front of the porch.

By then, I had joined Sarang outside. Together we calmed the dogs and wondered aloud if the fire was blowing up on the other side of the ridge. There was no hint of wind in the heavy night air, but we knew the fire could create its own microburst of intense wind speed and directional changes.

I blinked. Still disoriented from my brief respite, I thought the leggy officer emerging from the patrol car looked like my old college roommate. Impossible, since the girl I remembered had been the rowdiest, rudest, and most fun girl from Hana town. She would never have made it as a cop.

"Sorry if I woke you. The telephone and power companies shut this area down a couple hours ago."

Slack-jawed, I stared at the woman.

"Hey, Aloha. Sarang said you were coming home. Thanks for the Christmas letter." Her sarcasm ripped through the night like another lightning storm.

It was Lindy wearing the uniform. Was she hurt that I hadn't kept in touch? *Sheesh, time to let go of your abandonment issues.* I said this in my mind. Aloud I said, "I don't do Christmas cards." Responding to the accusation was easier than commenting on Lindy's occupation.

"Gee, I was hoping that was the reason you'd ditched me as your friend." For a moment, she focused on scratching Wharf's head. Then she inhaled and said, "So, Aloha, sorry to intrude on your vacation, but, we need your skills to assist our department."

"What the ... ?" I sure didn't see any use for my particular skills in a forest fire. "What's the deal, Lindy?" I also sent subliminal what's-the-deal-vibes to Wharf—Mr. Loyalty. Not!

"You're a Public Safety Diver, right?" Lindy read the title from her little spiral notebook. "My boss says we need your skills. Diving fatality. Apparent drowning victim. Photograph the scene. Behind the dam."

Lindy paused for a moment to step across Wharf. He looked up adoringly at his new friend. It looked like I had lost them both.

I had first met Lindy the year my family had come to Hana to visit Auntie Ruth. We'd hated each other immediately. She had been a scruffy little Tomboy. I was a little bit of a kiss ass ... even then. In her teens, she'd blossomed to Barbie-doll proportions. She looked Hawaiian, but since she was adopted, her true heritage was fuzzy. Her adoptive white parents brought her to Hana, the last bastion of old Hawai'i, to help her find her culture.

In college, when she paraded from one classroom to the next in the shortest shorts, guys would almost stampede to make contact with her. She'd developed her own subculture. I still remembered the words of Kāne, another Nooner brother. "Man, she's got legs all the way to the ground." Of course, Kāne—the deity, not the Nooner—had been the god of procreation. It made a certain kind of sense that he'd notice. A knowing look had passed between him and his twin brother Kanaloa, who had merely purred, "Oh yeah!"

In my own mind, I was big in the wrong places, and small in the important ones. Who needed a boring *haole*, when they could admire someone exotic? It was years before I realized that being blonde wasn't all-bad. By then, I'd also gotten to know Lindy. I had assumed our friendship had survived college and my running-away-from-Maui years. Maybe I was wrong. For some reason, Lindy was ticked off—and she needed a favor. I thought this a bad combination.

"Lindy, I can't leave Sarang's place. I'm only here to help her defend the cabin from the fire. I can't drop everything to shoot pictures of a corpse. Besides, I'm on administrative leave."

Lindy just kept scratching Wharf, as he melted onto her feet. Then she said, "The victim is Mallory Deems. Mallory Kila Deems. My boss already got it approved from your boss. The cell tower's out because of the fire, so she couldn't call you herself. Get your gear."

Inside I cheered. I have nothing against the phone company. Aloud, I said, "So she's gone?" You see, my little 'friend' Mallory Kila, who had succeeded in making that portion of my childhood spent in her presence so miserable, had trumped that action by marrying my former fiancé, Nate Deems. Shortly after Brother Love died, Nate dumped me due to the death-scene photo scandal.

Chapter Six

"Sarang," I turned to my sister, "I'm sorry, but I need to do this." I grabbed my purse. I knew that Sarang held no fond memories of Mallory Kila Deems, or her mother.

"I thought you couldn't dive anymore," her protective nature awakened.

"As long as I take out my hearing aid I'm good. My audiologist said the tissue damage has healed, even though I'll never get all my hearing back.

"Well then, be sure to take plenty of water with you. We don't need two UH Maui alumni plugging up the dam." She hugged me and pushed me away almost simultaneously.

Apparently, Lindy still knew me well. She didn't comment. She didn't even flinch. "We need to get going," she said. "Do you know how to get to the boat launch above the dam?"

I ignored the jab. "Yeah, I'll meet you up there. I've got four tanks of compressed air in my car and two sets of gear."

"Aloha," Lindy said softly, "you'll probably see Nate there. Let me know if I need to draw my sidearm." To augment the sad joke, she flipped open the two snaps that secured her Smith and Wesson 4566. Snake had the same gun, a stainless steel semi-auto. A rubber grip replaced the hard plastic one the gun came with. I knew from my training that almost every time an officer needs to draw a weapon, it's in a hurry. Lindy housed the four-inch barrel with Tritium sights—three dots that glow in the dark for night accuracy—in a class-three duty holster, a rating established by the difficulty in disarming the wearer, and the preferred style worn by patrol officers. Man, I really had learned a lot at that reserve academy.

In response to Lindy's quip, I said, "For me or for him?"

"Definitely for you. You know the old, 'There's nothing worse than a woman scorned' routine? And girlfriend, you were totally scorned."

Despite the grave situation, I could hear the glee in Lindy's voice. Maybe I hadn't lost two best friends after all. Lindy still had her sense of humor, and Wharf had moved over to sit on my feet.

Wharf and I both rehydrated before climbing back into the car. There was nothing worse for a diver than dehydration as a factor in decompression sickness, the malady commonly known as the bends.

We hopped in Buffy to follow Lindy in her cruiser. I continued to share my story with Wharf since he'd refocused on me now that Lindy was away.

"One summer," I told him, "when I was in third grade, the camp counselor asked who had been whispering during quiet time and Mallory pointed at me."

I didn't bother to tell him that had been the first of a thousand slivers she'd stuck under my nails. I glanced in the rearview mirror. It looked like he was listening with only one ear.

"I hate liars, especially those who lie to avoid punishment."

Wharf knew that. Other than the food thing, he is inherently honest.

Over the years, whenever we'd been teamed together at summer camp, Mallory rode to success on the backs of the rest of us. I would create posters for a project. Someone else would write the report. Mallory would do the presentation, implying that she'd done all the work. I had heard that in high school she partied harder than most. Often spending halftime in the parking lot during any sporting event, and then working the room at the dance afterward. What a man-eater!

Why I tried to emulate that lifestyle even briefly in college is a question best left for a professional. I wouldn't have met Eddie otherwise, so

I guess it wasn't all bad.

"Stupid. Stupid. Stupid." I made my famous grimace. Wharf blinked. Sometimes I needed more than a blink as conversation. I wanted to call Eddie. *Errr!* With no cell tower, no phone at Sarang's, and no time to stop, my thoughts returned to Mallory.

In college, I rarely saw her since I wasn't one of the popular crowd or a volunteer at the hospital, where Mallory candy-striped. Yet, we had both gone to the same university and she had married my boyfriend. Granted, she and Nate didn't have a relationship until her mom showed him the photos she took. That's when he—and the rest of the world it seemed—found out about my nude modeling. It incensed him. We argued and his embarrassment superseded his loyalty to me. I didn't blame him... until he hooked up with Mallory.

You see, Nate had been raised in a strict religious home. He consistently applied his Christian beliefs to his own actions. Although he didn't usually drink more than the occasional beer on a hot summer evening, after he saw those photos, he tried to drown his anger with me. He woke up the next day in Mallory Kila's bed. Three months later, she was Mrs. Nathaniel Deems. I hadn't wanted to hear about either of them since. Sarang, a stickler about never gossiping, willingly complied.

As I drove, I realized that this place would never be home again. It didn't matter that I knew every bend in the rutted road by heart. My feelings for Hana are hard to define.

To break my negative thoughts, I began to hum one of my favorite Henry Kapono songs, the soft steady melody numbing my brain. Before I knew it, I was back at the Hana Highway. Turning west, I goosed the accelerator and began climbing again, this time toward the dam at one of Maui Power and Electric's first stabs at hydropower.

My anxiety seemed to increase with the altitude. I could see the orange glow from the fires still burning on Honoma'ele Ridge and beyond. The road to Hana, famous as a journey and a destination, was deserted. This thought was a metaphor for Hana and its schizophrenic existence. Locals and non-Hawaiians lived in each other's worlds. In the 1800s, the area was open to homesteading. Quite a trick even then.

"We'll take your land, give you some other land, promise you peace, and promise to meet all your needs. And, by the way—we'll be giving some of that new land away."

People think today's government is dirty. Of course, back then they thought in terms of Manifest Destiny.

Now, the Hawaiians want to govern their land and people. The land, long inhabited by generations of others who lacked then, and even now, regard in many cases for Hawaiian cultural rules and traditions, was locked in modern law.

It's always about rules.

My mind jumped to diving rules. Never hold your breath. Never dive alone. Plan your dive. Dive your plan. *Blah, blah, blah.* I'd been doing it too long to give the rules a second thought.

Instead, I began making my mental checklist before doing a body recovery. That I would be photographing a dead body caused me some ambivalence, but it was part of the job. Certainly, I'd wanted to avoid Mallory on this junket. Maybe this was predestined, maybe just bad timing.

"Hey, Wharf, you in the mood for music?" The first song that came to my mind was *Ding Dong the Witch Is Dead*. When I reached the chorus "… *sing it high, sing it low…* " Wharf joined me with a howl. I considered few people inherently bad, and Mallory was one of them. My second reason for helping Lindy was to see for myself that this horrid person had spoken her last lie. So much for me being Miss Nicey-Nice-Nice.

At Wai'anapanapa Road, I turned onto the dead end. The road edged the utility company's offices and hydroelectric power plant, and then wound up past them to where the reservoir became a stream again.

Another road serviced the other side of the plant and the *taro* farms below.

I decelerated before I passed the power plant, remembering the chickens living in the Bermuda junipers alongside the road. It might not make me queasy to photograph a body, but I sure didn't want a road kill chicken on my conscience.

In another hundred yards, I arrived at the boat ramp parking lot. The manmade lake was normally a haven to Peacock bass fishers since there are only six natural lakes in all of Hawai'i. Hawaiians can fish year-round in a subsistence fishery, while non-Hawaiian fishers look forward to spring and fall seasons. This year I'd heard the predicted catch was slim to nil. No doubt, there would be an outcry that this should be a good reason to breach the new hydroelectric plant dam and increase the *taro* farms' water supply. The "breach the dam, don't breach the dam" chorus would be in full throat.

In an instant, I remembered one of the many lectures Brother Love had given me. "If they want to preserve the *taro* farms, they must preserve the water."

I wondered how the fires might further degrade the crop's riparian system. Less vegetation equals more runoff, which equals more sedimentation, which is not good for the *lo'i*. I could not resolve the conundrum. How do you fight Mother Nature and lightning strikes? Of course, the Wai'anapanapa Dam had tamed the river. Maybe the powers-that-be would tame the fire. Yeah, that would happen the same day that they undid their other inept environmental blunders. Sometimes it was hard for me to accept my lot as a public employee.

Although I was positive that there was not a fishery open in August, the boat ramp this evening resembled opening day—at night. A cop car blocked the entrance to the park, its lights flashing red, white, and blue reflections across the lake. A military invasion might have had fewer support staff and vehicles. Even with my window down, I heard no chatter over the radios. It was typical for a small force like this to go off the air during an investigation so that the local scanners couldn't beat them to the next-of-kin.

"Hi, I'm Aloha Aquilae...Jones," I said, smiling at the man guarding the entrance. Where had that little slip-of-the-tongue come from? Funny, I hadn't had trouble with my name change until now. "Lindy Somers has asked that I photograph the scene."

He looked at me as though I'd just been rubbed out of a magic teapot. I thought he was attractive, too. Unfortunately, the middle-aged officer—probably a couple decades from the academy—reminded me of my job. The racial profiling accusation made me furious. Though my fists clenched, I vowed to keep my professional demeanor in command. After checking my ID, the uniformed cutie-pie directed me to the action.

Getting out of my muscle car, I rolled down the windows and didn't lock the doors—even a mellow-yellow pooch would give someone second thoughts about rummaging through the vehicle. Ahead of me, several people leaned over the hood of an unmarked patrol car studying a set of blueprints. Lindy was in the midst of the group and signaled me over.

"Chief, this is Aloha Jones," Lindy said, directing my attention to a man who looked like a dark version of my dad—ex-military and built on a foundation of patriotism. He could model for a granite statue. Tall and lean, he held himself straight, looking directly at me. I wondered if the lines on his face were from a sense of humor or a permanent scowl. He reached out to shake my hand.

"Thanks for coming out, Mrs. Jones. I'm Chief Dhong. Understand you've had some experience in this type of thing."

Sheesh, Lindy must have told him a lot if he knew I was a missus once, a long time ago.

"Call me Aloha." I handed him my business card. "All Lindy told me was that you thought you had a drowning victim. What's the scoop?"

He grimaced. "I hope you don't still have ties to the media."

"No, no media ties," I scowled back at him. Was this because I'd said scoop? On the other hand, was this about the Brother Love photos? Everything inside me clenched. I'd learned the size of the force did not necessarily dictate the quality of the investigation. Up to this point, I'd assumed that Chief Dhong could lead the investigation with the skill and abilities of the best. Now I wondered.

"Lindy was first on the scene, dispatched to the dam at 0200 hours, and she requested an investigator. We're a small force and don't have a designated detective," he said. He then pointed to the man I'd recently met at the roadblock. "Although Haspin lateral transferred with 'dick' training."

I assumed he meant detective—really—but I still bit my tongue.

Chapter Seven

Haspin, the man to the chief's right, stuffed a wad of chewing tobacco into his cheek, then closed the lid on his tin. He brushed his hand on his uniform and held it out in greeting.

"Howzit? I hear you're a local girl." He made it appear that he didn't remember our earlier interaction at the checkpoint. I didn't believe it for a minute.

Concerned that the body was still intact—since I could hear the dam's turbines running in the distance—I ignored his implied question. The guy was probably being friendly, and exercising his "dick" muscles. Either way, I chose to stick with my job, although it wasn't yet clear what that entailed.

"Nice to meet you. Where's the body?"

Across the hood of the car, an older man cleared his throat.

Chief Dhong introduced me. "Aloha, this is Garry Daniels. He's the chief civil engineer with the utility company." To the other man, Dhong said, "Gar, Aloha is part of the investigation and she'll do the body recovery. Please be candid about the circumstances." Chief Dhong was polite but firm in his advice to Daniels, whose eyes met Dhong's in a silent plea.

Judging by his appearance, I guessed that the utility's executives were on vacation. Even at midnight, Daniels didn't fit my notion of an engineer. I could almost hear the fashion police booking him: "Listen buster, never wear cut-off jeans with black socks and loafers." The retro surfer aloha shirt didn't help the ensemble.

Running his fingers through a nasty comb-over, I could tell the engineer wished he were back in his control room. I figured he must spend a lot of time there since he was pale enough to glow in the dark.

Reaching across the hood, I extended my hand to the engineer. "Mr. Daniels, you probably don't remember me, but I sure remember you." His right eye started to twitch. I added, "Our science camp toured the dam during construction. I loved it when you showed us the Jacob's ladder. It really helped me to understand the power of electricity."

The Jacob's ladder or spark gap was 15,000 volts of electricity, arching up and down, between two wires. Daniels hauled it out for every "dam tour" as he had joked. I'd visited the dam again in college and even then, I had seen him as old. Now I realized that he'd probably been about my current age back then. These many years later, he had to be thinking retirement.

Our mutual fascination with the Jacob's ladder relaxed Daniels enough for him to say, "Until management arrives, I'm representing the utility in this unfortunate accident. Naturally, we want to keep the information limited. The person trespassed, but we don't want to press charges."

"Press charges?" Dhong's face registered surprise at Daniels' statement. "Gar, how in the world can you press charges on a dead body?"

It seemed his bosses at the utility had told him that a great offense is the best defense. Nobody wanted a corpse on his or her employment record. He straightened his fish-themed tie and stood at his full height of a few inches under six feet, posturing for his own defense.

I did the same and met him eye to eye. "Listen, if I'm going to get these shots tonight, I need to get going. Any volunteers?" It was kind of a rhetorical question. I figured that if they had someone, they wouldn't have tracked me down. Rescue divers dive alone all the time. It's one of those "do-what-I-say, not-what-I-do" things.

My only responses were an assortment of shifty glances from one face to another.

"Let's check these drawings one more time," Daniels hedged. At this rate, the investigation would continue into the next year. Dhong didn't seem the type to let an investigation simply evolve, but he sure wasn't pushing hard for a quick conclusion. I either needed some answers or to plan a morning dive.

"Uh, Chief, I'm confused. It's no problem not to include me in the investigation, but if you want me to shoot the scene, I need to get on it." Trying to be professional, yet flexible, I hoped this would ease the tension I felt as the group huddled around the patrol car. The desire to fit in clung to me like a wet T-shirt.

"You're right. The body was discovered after midnight, no point in dragging her out in the daylight." Dhong glanced at his watch, which prompted the rest to do the same. It was already three-thirty in the morning. The sun would blink over the ridge in just a few hours.

"The night operator of the control room was scanning his security monitors when he noticed something blocking the camera at the viewer—it's not uncommon." Dhong said with a nod to Daniels. "So he went down to check it out so he could file a work order on the obstruction. He said he got a little nauseous, and thinks he passed out when he saw the victim wearing scuba gear pressed against the glass. One of her hoses was hooked on the structural crossbars. It was obvious she was dead. Once he pulled himself together, he called Daniels, who instructed the man not to contact the police until he got here."

I could see that the investigation had bogged down even before the police arrived. I calculated that Mallory had already been in the water at least three hours. If this were true, she'd have limited rigor. No more of her ridiculous parade waves.

"Lindy told me the victim is Mallory Deems. Is that correct?" I unconsciously drummed my fingers on the cruiser's hood, *"Ding, Dhong, the witch is dead."*

Dhong frowned at Lindy and said, "Yes, Mallory Kila Deems. We've tentatively identified her. That car with all the bumper stickers," he pointed to a new Prius, "is registered in her name. As soon as we recover the body, we'll bring in the husband. I'm surprised he's not here yet. Another officer went to pick him up when I sent Lindy to your place."

I felt a flutter in my chest—stupid heart. Probably an aneurism.

Referring to his notes, Dhong said, "In addition to the underwater photos, we'll shoot the area between the car and the water, so we don't miss anything."

"I'd like an overhead line strung from the entry zone to the viewing area on the dam," I said. "I'll hook a carabiner to the line and sweep the entire course along the bottom. Maybe we can find out what she was doing here." I pointed to her location on the drawing. "Once on site, I'll go into the overflow tunnel with a safety line. I'd like to have someone standing by at the bottom with a radio in case the victim breaks loose and shoots through. We also need someone in the viewing area with a radio. I'll carry a slate. If I need anything, I'll write on it for the inside observer to read."

Dhong listened closely, making notes on his incident report pad. "We can't use radios," he said, as an afterthought. "Someone called in a bomb threat about an hour ago. They said the device had an electronic trigger. Might be a hoax, might not, probably a crack-pot muddying the waters." Dhong had just dropped his own bomb.

I guess his pun was unintended. I let it pass. The bomb was another matter. "Did you search?"

Haspin answered. "We did a walk through. I don't want to risk something being missed and detonating with a radio transmission. Don't worry." Then he smiled and patted my shoulder.

Like that made me feel better.

"What's the situation at the body?" I asked. My tummy was starting to make funny gurgling sounds.

Daniels, with his eyes on the prize, was the first to break the stark silence. He flipped through the blueprints until he found the viewing room's structural details. Pointing to them he said, "She's hung up on one of these cross-ties. According to this, they're spaced every ten feet along the tunnel. There's also one at each end. She's down about thirty feet from the first one. You'll need to make sure you don't get hooked-up the same way."

I sure wasn't looking to spend eternity with Mallory, so I took his warning to heart. Above us, the wires carrying hydroelectric generated power hissed and hummed.

"I don't suppose the turbines are shut down, are they?"

"Well, no, Jones, they're not," Daniels chided. "But, believe me, if we thought there was any danger to the turbines because of your diving, we'd have shut them down." He paused to scratch his nether region, then added, "No matter how much it would cost in lost electricity sales." Daniels seemed oblivious to the potential effects of the turbines on *my* body, especially as he struggled with his own. It looked like a crazy version of tug-a-war.

"There's pretty good water flow through the tube," Garrison added. "You're looking at about three knots of current. Of course, at the turbines, the water flows at a rate of over 115,000 gallons per second, but you shouldn't get near them."

I had no idea how to relate that last figure to my dive. I had no plans of getting near the turbines. However, a three-knot current could easily pull off my gear. I was already concerned about the dive's risks. This unique underwater environment would zap my air consumption and influence my dive profile. Considering this and my experience in underwater rivers, I let them know my safety measures.

"Okay, I'll rig a pulley and a harness for the recovery. Is there anything we can attach to on the back of the dam?" Again, a mix of uncomfortable looks was the response.

"Yeah," said Haspin. "According to Garry, you can hook up to the gantry crane in front of the water intake passages. They have one in front of the third tainter gate from the left."

He noted our confusion at the term. "A tainter gate's the radial arm floodgate used in dams and canal locks to control water flow."

Dhong chose this moment to regain control. "I'd like you to bring the body out here. There aren't any other areas along the back of the dam conducive to a recovery, even with a boat. We'll post someone on top of the dam to relay communications once you're on the surface. The coroner should be here by then."

As I returned to my car, Lindy joined me at the trunk.

"I'll go in with you." Lindy's voice bespoke her uncertainty.

"Whatever Dhong wants is fine with me." I didn't want to overstep my bounds with the local department. I had enough issues on the job already.

"After you left, he asked for volunteers. Haspin doesn't dive, but I got certified a couple years ago." She lowered her voice slightly in embarrassment. "I don't dive much in freshwater though, and never in a cave environment, and never a body rescue. Other than that, I'm good to go."

This was a bad idea, but I didn't want to make her mad again. The little people-pleaser, want-to-fit-in-person in my soul jumped to respond. "You'll do fine."

I couldn't help but think of the old legend about this area. The story is that a Hawaiian princess with a jealous husband hid with her maid in the Wai'ānapanapa Caves. After swimming through a water-filled lava tube, they sought sanctuary on a dry ledge inside the cave. A reflection on the water of her *kāhili*—her royal emblem—revealed the women's refuge. The husband killed them both, leaving the water flowing red. The legend says that when the waters flow red they represent the earth's rage by spilling its blood.

"Do you have a spare set of gear?" she asked.

I got all shifty-eyed and looked in the trunk. I'd already told her I did. Even to Haspin, "the trained dick," the answer was obvious. "Looks like she does to me," he answered on my behalf.

I doubted anything I had would fit her well, but I was willing to have her stretch my spare wetsuit in a new direction. The buoyancy compensator vest was not a big deal, so I figured it would all work out. I had changed into my swimsuit at the cabin. Lindy performed a quick-change behind the cruiser's door.

"Aloha, it sounds like all your dreams have come true." Lindy said, mid-jiggle. "Great job, no husband."

"Maybe I should have set the hoop higher," I said as I installed my digital camera in its underwater housing. In my life, people, place, and technology had drastically changed in the past few years. Then I thought about her implication.

"It was love for a while," she said.

This time I heard a challenge in her voice. Lindy had met Eddie. She knew how close we had been... at first. I didn't want to tell her about what he was doing these days. I responded, "Yeah, something like that." No way was I going to take the bait.

Instead, I rummaged around in the Mustang. Since I hadn't unloaded anything but Wharf at Sarang's, I moved my gun into the locked case and into the trunk. In my career in the Coast Guard and again in my reserve law enforcement class, I had learned three things: A gun is always loaded, don't point it at anything you don't want to shoot, and don't yell, "Stop, or meet your maker!" at the range. As Meatloaf said, "Two out of three ain't bad." Nobody has a sense of humor anymore.

Unfortunately, the first time I tried to fieldstrip a Glock I shot a hole through the wall. That never happened again. I made it my policy to make a mistake only once. These days I figure a big dog and a loaded gun keep me out of the victim pool. Nothing keeps me from being a klutz.

I wondered if someone had helped Mallory into that same pool or if her death resulted from a combination of simple mistakes—mistakes an expert would call stupidity. I'd never pictured Mallory as intelligent as much as cunning, and indeed manipulative. Yet I didn't think of her as stupid either.

"Lindy, what was the scoop with Mallory? Were she and Nate happily married?" I tried hard to sound casual. I had become much too emotional back in the day. Only recently had I realized how well the passing years had eased the pain of my failed romances. I had come to embrace the "wait until you're fifty to get married again" school of thought.

Of course, I also thought there ought to be a parenting test. You can't drive a car without a license. What business do you have attempting to guide a two-year-old or, worse, a teenager—in my opinion, two far more dangerous vehicles—without proper training?

While I considered possible questions for the parenting test, I leaned into my trunk and rummaged around for a spare water bottle, while Lindy told me about Nate's daughter. With my semi-blown hearing, I failed to hear Lindy's entire report on Nate and Mallory's marriage.

"Their daughter, Missy, was an angel. Half the town showed up for the funeral." Lindy gazed toward the sky. The haze filled the night. No stars were in sight. Breathing deeply, Lindy turned to me. "But, Sarang told you all about that, didn't she?"

Chapter Eight

I couldn't speak. I could barely think. I had no idea that Nate and Mallory had lost a child. Despite my nearly non-existent marriage, let alone never having been a mother, I knew no parent was ever prepared to lose a child, at any age. That Missy was so young intensified the tragedy. For the first time, I felt sad for both Nate and Mallory.

"What happened?"

"Aloha, haven't you been listening? Don't make me go through it again. Every time we think about Missy, it makes us so mad!" Lindy pressed the heels of her hands against her eyes, then, ran her fingers through dark bangs. Taking another deep breath she said, "Missy—well, her real name was Melissa—died when she was five. She had cancer but her treatment looked like it was working. Then one day she faded… in a matter of hours. Nate and Mallory's marriage was never the same. Rumor had it that divorce was imminent."

I could understand why. What I didn't understand was how Mallory and Nate could have had a child to begin with. While we were dating, he told me he was sterile because of some childhood trauma. I had decided by the time I was twelve that I didn't want children, so he seemed the perfect partner.

Moreover, who was the other half of the "we" Lindy mentioned? Did she have an imaginary friend or a split personality? While listening to her, I had stripped to my swimsuit and squeezed into my three-millimeter neoprene wetsuit. Sweat ran off my temples, under my jaw and between my breasts. Even skinny women break into a sweat in this process, and I was a little more "Rubenesque" than Lindy.

Lindy's eyes seemed to widen and a grin formed. My back was to the car's open doors but I had heard the thud. I looked down to see Wharf laying spread eagle upside down on the ground where he'd fallen from the car. When he sleeps, he likes to have his head hanging off the edge of the bed, seat, or stair. He keeps his front feet tucked up under him, and then he mule kicks one hind leg out behind for quick starts. About one time out of ten, his silky fur and jaunty style work against him and he slips from his perch. He always acts as if it's "no big deal and meant to do that". He never worries about fitting in.

I tried to cover for him by getting him outfitted. "Wharf. Hup, hup." My big friend scrambled up and headed toward the tires of the patrol car. Lindy still appeared amused. I offered him a shred of canine modesty and looked away as he relieved himself.

"I guess…I know…what he thinks…of the Hana…Police Department. Sometimes…I feel…the same," Lindy snorted, her words erupting between bounces, as she tugged the zipper over her chest.

As she finished, Haspin approached us. "Hey, Sistah, need help wit da suit? I hold the front together for ya."

Lindy's back was to him and he couldn't see her flush.

"Thanks Haspin. I've got it handled," she said, fastening the Velcro clasp on the neoprene collar. She unpacked gear and self-consciously set it up while Haspin continued. "We want you two to bring da girl back here for the coroner. Once you done, you can hit da bar. They open at six."

Still working a wad of chew with his tongue, he raised his eyebrows and attempted a provocative smile. He resembled a stroke victim with that puffy-faced look like Alec Baldwin on a bad day.

I couldn't figure out why Lindy was putting up with his harassment. I knew Title VII by heart. "Unwelcome sexual advances, requests for sexual favors, and other verbal or physical conduct of a sexual nature constitutes sexual harassment when submission to or rejection of this conduct explicitly or implicitly affects an individual's employment, unreasonably interferes with an individual's work performance or creates an intimidating, hostile or offensive work environment."

I figured Haspin knew it too.

"Hey, Haspin." I lowered my voice and glanced around, silently urging him into my personal space. He leaned close enough so I could whisper in his ear. "You know the great thing about smokeless tobacco?"

He squinted and shook his head.

"You probably won't have to worry about lung cancer. That chew gets to you so fast, that you'll be busy having your jaws, lips, and chin removed. Of course, if it metastasizes, I guess it could kill you from your lungs—but it's probably a toss-up."

It was a horrible thing to say and I knew it. Somehow, I just felt like I needed to defend Lindy. Even though she was a cop and no doubt competent, she had once been my best friend. I knew she struggled with belonging too.

He spat tobacco juice on my ankle.

I had it coming.

Coughing slightly, he feigned an apology without eye contact.

To Lindy I said, "Well, we've hit a new level of low here in Hana, haven't we?" I leaned over to buckle my buoyancy compensation device onto my aluminum tank while Haspin walked back to the group.

"I've already filed a grievance. He was counseled, I was counseled, and that's the end of it." Lindy turned and promptly screwed the regulator onto the tank valve upside down. When she realized her mistake, she slumped on the edge of the bumper, head back and her eyes on the smoky sky.

"Sorry, Aloha. Maybe I'm not up to this."

"Relax and don't sweat it. We'll review as we go. Let's start our check.

You're going to love my transport system."

I had my gear ready to go and said one word to Wharf. "Harness." He stepped around the gear and stood quietly while I slid his nylon harness over his massive cranium, past his shoulders, and snapped it closed across the yellow fur on his chest.

"Poor puppy," Lindy said, as she hefted her own gear over her shoulder.

"He likes it."

"Really?" Her head tilt and tone told me it was a rhetorical question.

"He does." I thumbed the car's lock and held the handle as I shut the door.

"Wharf, get up." He carried his load with a steady force. His head and tail high, he gave every appearance of an elegant porter. He had learned this skill in only a day. He loved to work, to be involved. However, it took extensive training to keep him at the water's edge while I dove. Sometimes he couldn't control himself. Like all of us, his hardwiring sometimes overshadowed his training.

We paused near the men huddled around the set of drawings. "Chief, we're geared up. Any last words?" Lindy asked. Dhong shook his head as we trundled to the water's edge.

I was losing faith in the local police force. I lost faith in the mission as I stood at the top of the grooved concrete launch ramp. Instead of ripples lapping at my feet, the waterline was a good twenty vertical feet below us, well past the ramp's base.

"Where'd the water go?" Dumb question on my part. I knew it went down the river. I just didn't know why.

"Combination of draw down for the *taro* and the increased power needs." Lindy said, with no apparent opinion on either item.

"What increased power needs?" I asked to keep Lindy's mind off the dive. Hana isn't the epicenter of industry on Maui. This made no sense to me.

"The utility sold the power to Lahaina. This is their peak season." This time Lindy's emotion was clear—disgust. Some people didn't get that the tourists were necessary and welcome sources of income and that the Islands didn't close the doors the day after they had arrived themselves. There really weren't many true Hawaiians—or locals—for that matter.

Nevertheless, I had no time to ponder the problem. We'd reached the bottom of the ramp and the limit to Wharf's assistance. He settled down to await my return, behaving with responsibility... so far.

Lindy and I traipsed to the low water's edge. Facing each other, we ran through our pre-dive checklist. While we had geared up, the overhead line was shot and secured. We each clipped a carabiner to it, rubbed spit in our masks to help keep them clear, and exchanged the "Okay" sign. I felt like a piece of bait on a hook. I hate encumbrances while diving, but this situation called for such a precaution. The carabiner was the perfect tool for the job. The D-ring with a spring catch on one side commonly used by mountaineers made it easier to release than a tied attachment.

Wharf abandoned his grownup demeanor and starting whining. This wasn't just a water thing. He's as dependent on me as I am on him. Being a pack animal—this time not the carrying kind, but the group kind—he despises solitude. Unlike him, I'm not afraid of being alone, but of loneliness. For him, the mere state of being alone is foreign. I should have left him with Sarang. I gave him a little wave. He yawned in response. That's the same as saying "F-you" in dog.

As I stepped into the reservoir, guilt filtered through my psyche while cool water percolated inside my wetsuit. When I was waist deep, I pulled on my fins. Lindy did the same.

"Let's surface swim a ways, then we'll drop down to twenty feet before we follow the bottom. We'll survey on the way back. Stay close, and relax." I smiled with my eyes. Lindy seemed comfortable and focused.

Even though the water was cooler than my body temperature, it felt good to be neutrally buoyant again. Gradually, the thin layer of water inside my wetsuit was warming. The lights on the dam illuminated the water. I was in my element.

I held the camera close to my chest as I swam toward the huge concrete monolith. A slight current tugged me toward the far side. As I began my descent, I carefully squeezed my nose to equalize my air passages to the water pressure. At ten feet underwater, my dive light reflected off the sediment in the water. When I was about five feet from the overflow opening, I turned to Lindy and again gave her the "Okay" signal, which she returned. The current pressed us to the concrete back of the dam.

I clipped a short line to the rods across the entrance and photographed its construction. I signaled to Lindy that I was ready to make my descent. My submersible pressure and depth gauge read 2800 psi. I clipped it back on to my buoyancy vest. The last thing I needed was loose gear hooking on anything on my way down. When I pushed off from the concrete wall, the current pulled me through the grate, making kicking unnecessary. Its force steadily propelled me forward.

The water in the dark underwater tunnel tried to swirl and confuse me. Often in my life, I had felt that the wind was malevolent. This was this was the first time I felt the water had an ominous nature. In seconds, I rounded the bend where light from the viewing window flooded the space and I saw Mallory. My stomach lurched. Her eyes and mouth were open, her gaze blank, and her voice silent. Nonetheless, like all the victims I had recovered in the past, she called to me. It was the only reason I could accomplish these missions. I did it to answer their pleas: *Find me. Free me. Get me out of the water.*

A structural metal rod was wedged between her tank and its valve stem. I braced my fins against the steel grate to hold myself in place and hooked my harness to the rod. Then I steadied myself, grabbed my camera and got to work. Once I had shots from above, I eased through the bars and shot film from below. Mallory's arms and legs were askew, probably from struggling to get free. Her mask was gone and her regulator trailed below her like a kite in the breeze. The cool water had slowed the rigor process, allowing her limbs to wave freely.

Dang it, even in death, she still had that parade wave perfected.

I turned to the viewing window and signed "Okay" to the lanky, ruffled man inside. He looked like of Shaggy in Scooby Doo, but reminded me of someone else. No time for more thoughts about him. I needed to focus on the ultimate victim, as she had perfected that role so well in life. Finding her was easy. Now it was time to free her.

I hooked a harness and line to Mallory. It was simple releasing her valve from its entrapment, but tougher maneuvering her appendages through the grate. The water's velocity slapped her body against mine and I struggled to push her away. Never a big fan of hugging, this chance encounter was particularly distasteful. My security line grew taut as we slipped past the viewing windows and my tank slammed into the next set of tie rods. I frantically tugged on the return line. My safety line, the one hooked to Lindy's reel, went completely slack. It wrapped itself around me in a cold embrace in which I played a passive role. The phrase "death grip" ricocheted around in my skull.

A moment before, I worried that the coroner would throw a fit if the body exhibited postmortem trauma. Now I abused my own body to save us both. Instinctively, like a kid on the monkey bars, I wrapped my legs around the rods and grasped the webbed shoulder strap on Mallory's buoyancy vest.

Oh God! Oh God! Oh God! Oh God! My mind screamed. The steel's rough edges dug into the neoprene and then the flesh behind my knees. While I hung upside down in the concrete tube, I didn't have time to consider what had gone wrong. I didn't even focus on the pain and fear. Instead, I was mad. Mad at Lindy, at Mallory, at Brother, at Sarang, at

Snake, at Dhong, at Daniels, and at Haspin.

For once, I wasn't mad at myself.

This wasn't my first rodeo and I had come prepared. It took me just a few seconds to sort out the equipment and body parts. When I had everything secure, I pulled and kicked my way upstream along the secondary line I had clipped to the first set of rods I passed in my descent. Then I eased our bodies back through the first grate, using the line to make my way upstream. At the viewing window, I didn't stop to signal my problem. A glance told me that was a good choice as the area was empty. My safety and communication guy was gone. I used the light to check my air supply. I was down to 1200psi.

Kicking hard, it took me several minutes to reach the second grate. Once there, I again checked my air supply—down to 800 psi. Swimming against the current had caused me to use more air than usual and had cost me valuable time. My imagination tried to take control, to tell me to freak out. The little frightened girl in my head whimpered and tried to hide in the corner.

Instead, I exhaled fully and took a deep breath.

I did another strong swim to the final grate where I pulled myself and my dead dive buddy around the corner—no Lindy. All I had to do was hoist Mallory through the last grill and swim back to the ramp. Mallory's arms hung up a little in the process. To extricate her, I braced my feet on the rod and the concrete. I used all the pull I had to dislodge her fluid form. I counted this time as part of my safety stop at fifteen feet. Still, I didn't sprint to the surface. With my last breath, I ascended slower than my bubbles, exhaling the whole way.

As I broke the surface, I knew I didn't even have enough air in the tank to inflate my BCD. Without thinking, I pressed the auto-inflate on Mallory's and it whooshed. It hadn't dawned on me to check her air supply or use her air myself. I had assumed she'd run out hours earlier.

Now she buoyed me. Before I switched from my regulator to my snorkel, I inflated my BCD a breath at a time. Toward the boat ramp, I could see two separate heads bobbing in the water. One screaming and flailing, headed toward the shore, the other methodically paddling to her assistance.

Others rushed to join the paramedics waiting at the water's edge with a white body bag. Their attentions focused on Lindy, I knew they didn't notice me in the distance. I couldn't hear more than smidgens of speech above the turbine's continuous whine. With my lips clamped around the silicone mouthpiece, I kept sucking in the night air through my snorkel. Then I pushed my face back into the water, and began my slow swim back to the landing. This gave me time to calm my breathing and collect my thoughts.

Every hundred kicks I glanced up to check my course. In doing so, through my mask's glass lens, I witnessed a freeze-framed procession up the steep ramp. During my next hundred kicks, something brushed my trailing right arm. Were walking on water one of my skills I would have been sprinting to shore. As it was, my feet dropped and I yanked my mask down under my chin so I could better see what had brushed me. When I spun around in the water, a dark shape loomed in silhouette, inches from my face. Before my heart restarted, an enormous pink tongue bathed my face. Then I realized it was Wharf licking my tears.

Chapter Nine

When I got to the ramp, the paramedics hauled Mallory's corpse up to their gurney at its lip. Even from where I stood in the water, I could see them tugging the zipper on the front of her wetsuit. They attached a heart monitor to confirm her death. I could have saved them the trouble.

Their protocol completed, they pulled the bag over her body and closed it securely before they wheeled her to the ambulance. That zipper noise always makes me shudder.

They had stripped Mallory's scuba gear from her when we reached shore and laid it on the ground. I did the same with my own. Wharf dogged my every step until I urged him to back off.

When I scrambled up the ramp with my gear, I saw Lindy behind a second ambulance sucking on an oxygen mask. She dropped it when she saw me and stepped in my direction.

"Hey," Haspin startled me from behind. "You need a hand with that?" He grabbed Mallory's tank by the black plastic grip.

"Don't touch that!"

He dropped it as if it had just zapped him with a Taser. The tank clanked against a rock with a loud ping. I jumped back and shot him a dirty look.

"Didn't they teach you not to touch evidence?" I asked. I didn't even get into why it's a bad idea to drop a scuba tank on the rocks.

He returned my look but kept silent. Dhong had just begun his ascent up the ramp. I said, "Do you guys have a thumb drive I can download the photos onto?"

Haspin laughed. Dhong just shook his head and said, "You'll need to go by Nagasako's for printing."

Great, Nagasako's News. Not my biggest fans.

"Da line broke." Dhong said, as he looked toward the dam.

I held the frayed end up to him. Some fibers had ragged edges, some looked cut clean.

"Must have been something sharp at the first corner," Haspin said.

"Glad I ran a second line."

"Guess the saying's not true." Haspin again pulled a pinch from his tobacco can.

"What saying?" I had returned to shucking gear.

"'Dope on a rope.' I thought that's what they call rescue divers."

"Nope, that's what we call the guy on the other end."

Since he hadn't been involved, he didn't take it as an insult. Bummer.

Dhong, his arms folded across in chest, asked, "What do you think happened to her?"

An unconcealed shiver rippled up my spine. "I don't know."

"You knew her didn't you?" Haspin again inserted himself into the conversation.

Time to get going. I lifted my tank. Dhong took it from me. I followed him to Lindy's patrol car. Again, trying to respond to Dhong's question, I said, "I'm sure the coroner will discover the cause of death."

Haspin, continuing his own line of discussion and said, "Seems like you know just about everybody here. You 'friends' with the chief too?" He did the finger quote thing.

"Haspin—" In the gloom I could see Dhong's jaws tighten as though to stop himself from saying more.

We stopped at my car's trunk where my gear that Lindy had used lay stacked against the tire. I could see her in the front seat of her cruiser talking on her cell phone. It looked like the cell tower been repaired during my dive.

From behind me, Haspin's voice interrupted my thoughts. "I hope you don't let this affect your friendship."

"What?"

"You know, her leaving you down there."

I turned to him. "We both came back. She just got here ahead of me."

A deep "woof" punctuated the pause in conversation. Wharf wagged from behind Mallory's car. This time Lindy's voice distracted me. "Aloha, I'm so sorry. I...I don't know what happened."

I didn't have a chance to respond. All three of their radios toned. After listening to another officer request immediate backup at a domestic call, they hurried to their cars. I thought I heard the words *poi* and overdose. I had to assume my good ear was filling in the blanks for my bad ear and it had a sense of humor. Of course, to me, one bite of *poi* is an overdose. Despite having been born in Hawai'i, I am not a fan of the pasty carb. And truly, unless *taro* is cooked, it is indeed, poison. Hawaiians I know say the green foliage, also edible, has as many vitamins as spinach. I don't eat spinach either. I like to be consistent. Oprah might not eat anything white, but I had a rule against most things green.

As Lindy backed her cruiser around for a quick exit, she lowered her window and said, "Meet me for lunch tomorrow?"

"I'm here to help Sarang."

She didn't hear my response over the sound of Haspin's horn behind her. She grimaced and yelled, "I'll call you!" Then, all three cars sped from the parking lot and careened down the road, lights flashing, and their sirens silent.

The officer I had checked in with remained on scene, I assumed to guard Mallory's car. I tried to give him her dive gear. He radioed Dhong who told me to isolate it and bring it to the station later in the day.

Once I had everything loaded, I looked around for Wharf. Although daylight was beginning to show on the ridge, a few remaining lights at the boat ramp gently illuminated the fine steam rising above the reservoir, blending it with the smoke-laden night air. Still as a statue, I could see him sitting at the ramp's top edge, staring into the water. When I walked closer, I heard his sporadic whine.

I knew how he felt.

I could only speculate as to why Mallory had broken so many diving rules: Alone, in an overhead environment, with a strong current, and under-equipped since I didn't see a knife on her. Any one error could have been fatal, but certainly all of them contributed to her death. Little did I know.

Throughout the night, there had been no wind. Although the fires continued to burn through dense jungle, the flames hadn't moved any closer to Sarang's. Still, I felt guilty for being gone during her crisis. Inside the cabin, I found her in bed with Stinger on guard. Although the Chow Chow gave me the stink-eye, she stayed quiet.

As I nestled on to the couch with a crocheted afghan, I realized I hadn't seen Nate at the lake. Uh! I didn't want to give him a second thought. Instead, I wanted to call Snake. What's with that? Even with Wharf curled up on the floor next to the couch, I was homesick.

Sleep came with snail's speed and stayed less time than it took a drunk driver to sober up and get out of jail.

I woke up choking and my first thought was lung cancer. It wasn't easy calming my hypochondriacally induced tendencies when the acrid smell of burning vegetation blistered my throat. Panic struck as I tried to orient myself.

When I opened my eyes, I recognized the tongue and groove car decking above my head. Had I overslept? My watch said it was only seven o'clock, yet it was surprisingly warm for early morning. Was the cabin on fire?

With a quick inspection, I discovered myself alone. Neither my sister nor the dogs were in sight. I slipped on my flip-flops and hurried outside. As I opened the screen door, I heard helicopter rotors whirling beyond the ridge. An orange pall hung over everything in sight, my horizon limited by the dense smoke in the valley. A painful ache flared in my throat.

In the jungle of Sarang's backyard, I found Wharf asleep in the shade of the springhouse. Sarang and Stinger were inside, fiddling with something. Nothing on fire.

"Morning," I called from a safe distance outside the door.

"Good morning. How'd it go last night?" Sarang swallowed something as she closed the springhouse door. There was vegetative slurry on her lips. Clearly she did not share my "no green" rule. Around us, the sprinklers whirred in her garden.

"Got the job done." I always try to play down the danger of my job. I occasionally wonder how long it will last. I don't think my hypochondria is responsible for my consistent joint pain and backaches, not to mention my bad ear. I was surprised I wasn't hurting despite just a few hours couch time after a tough dive.

Time to get to work. "What do we need to do?" In addition to the helicopter noise, I could hear a bulldozer cutting a fire line.

"The fires passed us," Sarang said, as we walked back to the cabin.

"You're sure?"

"I guess I did all this for nothing." She waved her hand toward the downed timber. I could see a tremor in her movement. She was out of steam. It wasn't like her to view life in hindsight.

"Hey, I need to get to Nagasako's to transfer the images I shot and take the dive gear to the police department. Come with me." I paused, "Lindy asked me to meet her for lunch. That's flexible though, depending on what you need me to do here."

I scratched Wharf's head. While we walked, he tugged on my sleeve, trying to pull me into play. Stinger watched with a contemptuous look. I could tell she thought him a buffoon. Even she didn't realize looks could be deceiving.

"They're predicting some cloudiness today and cooling temperatures. This fire might burn itself out." My sister is a person whose glass is always half full. I wondered why she had called me here. Sarang was confident and capable in nearly any situation. Plus, she had close ties throughout the community.

Still, I was grateful, because her call motivated me to face my own personal misgivings. More importantly, it made me feel needed. Not having anyone depend on me other than Wharf was beginning to nudge at my psyche. It wasn't the biological clock ticking. That sucker was broken. I guess I just want to belong to a pack. Sometimes I think I understand the canine's social dynamic better than that of humans.

"I'd like to see for myself where the fire line is right now," I said, shaking off this new reverie. "How about driving around with me to see if we can get more information? Maybe Māko's is open and we can get some malasadas for breakfast." My stomach rumbled at the thought of the fried doughy pastry covered with butter, sugar, and cinnamon. Umm...

"I need to stop at the clinic anyway. It's so close to Nagasako's, we can ride together and check out the situation," Sarang said, while deadheading spent blooms on a native orchid.

A dozen butterflies dive-bombed in my stomach. Sarang believed in natural healing and remedies. A trip to the clinic was a rarity in her life. Knowing that my sister wouldn't readily share the reason for her visit, I chose to postpone my questions until after the office call.

"Sounds perfect. I'd like to see what's new around here," I fibbed. Although I felt secure in my lead role in the body recovery the previous evening, I wanted my sister at my side when I stepped back into Hana's "society".

Because I had parked my car behind hers, I drove the Mustang into town, leaving the dogs snoozing in the shade.

As I retraced my dusty tire tracks down the driveway, I told my sister about the previous evening's recovery. Although the more gruesome aspects wouldn't bother Sarang, I preferred not to share details. In any small town, but especially in Hana, I wouldn't want my comments inadvertently repeated—or worse, misquoted. On the other hand, I could tell Sarang anything, and it would never be repeated. She abhorred gossip, to a fault.

Although I believe the soul leaves the body at death, and that the remaining vessel is just that, others treat the deceased with mystic reverence. Hawaiians in particular hold great reverence for the bones, as they believe the bones retain a person's *mana*. Within Oceanic cultures, *mana* is the substance of which souls are created. A person could expand and increase his or her *mana* through earthly endeavors like art, dance, chant, meditation and healing.

Okay, maybe it isn't a faulty philosophy.

Chapter Ten

We rode comfortably in silence as the road transitioned to a smaller dirt lane over Hono'māele Ridge. As we reached the crest, visibility diminished. I slowed to avoid a collision with any firefighters. The grade was steep, running nearly parallel to the peak as it dropped to the valley floor, screened by the smoke shroud.

Jungle debris covered the ground. "Man, everything is tinder dry," I broke Sarang's private thoughts with my comment on the obvious.

The song, *I Am the God of Hell's Fire*, began playing in my brain. I had a foggy memory of singing it in college, tipsy and dancing with Lindy near a hot lava flow on the Big Island. Another brilliant choice unearthed. I had too many bad memories on this trip already. The song was stuck, but I willed the memory into oblivion and refocused on the terrain.

Although access to the community was restricted during the fire, once inside the boundaries, no one seemed concerned about who went where. The local post office parking lot was nearly empty as we passed it on our way to Māko's.

It seemed most of the locals had evacuated, with the remaining population appearing to be solely yellow-shirted firefighters. Each toted the requisite accessory for fire fighters—a Pulaski: the double-edged hand tool with an ax blade on one side and a pickax on the other. Two such visitors pushed through the restaurant's front door as I parked the now dusty Mustang. It chugged to a rough halt.

Māko's was to Hana what the pressroom is to the White House. It seemed that news as small as a scraped knee made the rounds of discussion. Māko himself was usually the center and source of the local fact and fiction passed around the tables. Although he used the iconic mako shark image on his sign, his name was the equivalent of rocky or rough. Funny how a little line over a vowel in Hawaiian can totally change the meaning of a word.

His wife, our Auntie Ruth, was the queen of the kitchen—her malasadas famous from Hilo to Honolulu. She'd married Māko late in life after exploring the rest of the world on her own. She found her true life's mate in Māko and her home in Hana. Only rarely did she leave the community these days. It would be too painful for her to be out of the gossip loop.

Tall, but with a heavy frame, Ruth still moved quickly. Long braids with hints of silver twined through them bounced in synchronous harmony with her body. Stopping inches away from me, totally disregarding my personal bubble, she smiled. Her beautiful white teeth contrasted against her dark round face and eyes. She is, was, and always will be a classic beauty. The extra years and pounds only add a sense of grace to her striking elegance.

As usual, she began in the middle part of a conversation, rather than at the beginning. "Are you thrilled?" Ruth hugged me and received a dirty look from Sarang. "Oops." She shrugged it off and restarted. "Come in and get some malasadas. I have a batch ready to cook." Stepping aside, Ruth herded us through the screen door.

Māko was at the counter pouring coffee and commiserating with the only other business owner on the south side of the river, Roy Ilima, better known as Cowboy Roy. The rest of the place was empty save for five men in matching yellow garb drinking coffee and stretching back in their chairs.

Cowboy Roy grinned. Although I'd known him for years, I didn't know how Sarang would respond to him. When he inherited the town's service station across the road from Māko's and renamed it Cowboy Roy's she pitched a fit. She thought it attempted to create humor at the expense of historic conflicts. Both he and the name stuck, but so did her resentment against him. Fortunately, their paths crossed infrequently. He hadn't aged a day since I had last seen him. He stood a good six feet tall, big in the chest, with thinning gray hair, a thick droopy mustache and a kind smile.

After I hugged Māko and Roy, Sarang and I joined them at the counter. The original laminate finish had worn through to the base color in front of the bar stools. I heard grease sizzling in the kitchen where Ruth dropped fresh dough into the deep-fat fryer. I moaned in my head. When I looked at the surprised faces of my friends, I realized my inside voice had sneaked outside again. I needed to put a latch on my mental screen door.

Māko, a walking advertisement for Ruth's food, moved the three-bowled rotating server with whipped margarine, cinnamon sugar, and store-bought guava jam in front of me. Seeing this, Ruth scampered out of the kitchen and snatched it away, saying, "Oh no you don't!" When she returned, she brought a cube of butter and some of her own homemade guava jam.

Both men rolled their eyes.

Māko looked at Roy and said, "Guess you need to leave town for a few years to get the good stuff around this joint." Roy nodded but didn't comment. He knew better than to mess with women when it came to pastry. Māko wrapped his bulky arm around his wife's waist and gave her a squeeze as he winked at Sarang and me.

Of course, the whole time Ruth was rattling off local news blips in my direction. "Kanaloa's wife left him for a woman biologist doing a study on noxious animals. Lindy is the new member of the police department. Oh, you probably saw her when you fished for Mallory. She and Nate were getting divorced, no point in telling you why." She took a breath. "Half the girls in the graduating class are pregnant. Only two big weddings on the horizon, though. Kāwika's back managing the *taro* cooperative."

Sarang kept frowning at her to no avail.

Kāwika? Kāwika Padriac? I hadn't seen him since high school. He was older and I'd had a huge crush on him. It still made my heart pitter-patter at the thought. Last I heard he had left Maui for the big city, fame and fortune. Before I could ask about him, I missed several more headlines.

Ruth blathered on. "Kū got hit on the head so hard he can't get a Coke out of the machine with a pocketful of quarters. Then Andi's son got arrested for cutting a brodie in the chief's lawn. 'Course, he apologized." She rolled her eyes.

Like hopping into a spinning jump rope, I said, "Did Dhong buy into that?"

"Yep, like a mongoose after eggs."

Māko added to her repertoire. "Joannie got arrested for doing a smash and grab at that art gallery in town."

Ruth stopped to appraise the info. "How'd you find that out?"

"Saw her at the clinic when I picked up..." He stopped mid-sentence when Ruth kicked him. "Uh, she was being treated for handcuff wounds."

I raised my eyebrows.

"The store owner couldn't hold her 'cause she was doing that girl slapping thing. They ended up cuffing one hand to the door and she purt near unhinged it. Haspin was not happy." Māko did a pantomime of hiking up his pants.

"I heard from Lindy that Haspin was lurking around her place. Course, she has her eye on his job."

Another breath.

"So, the harvest is down this year and the pickers are worried about losing overtime. They put together a marching group for parades to raise awareness, so they need travel money.

Roy pressed her reboot button when he asked, "Must color and ideology march in lockstep?" He always asked slightly odd, perhaps ironic questions. Was lockstep in reference to the marching band or was the ideology about the *taro* pickers? He had served in the first Iraq war and I had heard he suffered from PTSD. Of course, it could be he just saw the world differently. I didn't know.

"You refute racism with your heart Roy," Māko said. Sarang choked on her coffee.

Ruth went back to her update. "A bunch of dopers got together to party last weekend and one faction decided the other wasn't being friendly enough, so they took tin snips to one of the opposing crew's lips." She squeezed her hand in a cutting motion while she said, "Chich, chich, chich."

I shuddered. Small town crime, big city sick.

"Tin Snips gets worried that they'll return the favor, so he pulls out an AK-47 and starts shooting. Dhong found forty rounds in the neighbor's house." Apparently this wasn't shocking enough, since she added, "He reloaded twice!"

From the other side of the room we heard a firefighter exclaim, "No way!" We all turned to see what the ruckus was just in time to watch two young men pick up their packs and trot to the door. The others at the table paid the bill, then picked up their gear and followed their teammates.

"So much for business this morning," Māko harrumphed. "We might as well close up and leave along with everyone else." Untying his huge serving apron, Māko couldn't mask his disappointment that business was slow, or more accurately, non-existent. His dark eyes lost their sparkle when he turned the Open sign on the front door to Closed. There could not have been a worse time for us to finish our malasadas. With a guilty look at Sarang and Roy, I hoped one or the other would initiate the exodus.

Māko couldn't maintain his dark mood as he watched his closest friends squirm in their seats, wanting to leave, but not wanting to bring him down further.

"Git, all of you! Ruth and I are going to head home while the rest of you run around worrying about the fire. With what I heard from those boys that left, we'll be plenty busy this evening."

My curiosity always overwhelmed my manners. "Why will you be busy later, Māko?"

"Hunt Goldswaithe is flying in to declare this an emergency disaster area. I think that's been his goal all along. At least now he'll have it out of his system."

Māko laughed at his own joke, but the others bristled at having the new Secretary of the Environment on local lands. As the Hawai'i State Resource Commissioner, he had initiated numerous court cases against the towns using the environment as his hammer. Back then, he made every attempt to rob the Hawaiian people of their land and resource rights. A consummate butt-kissing bureaucrat, he had finally earned a cabinet position in the latest administration.

I knew Māko was right about being busy later in the day. Goldswaithe wouldn't be caught dead on the island without his retinue of handlers and press. No doubt, they would mob Māko's, as they would all want to be seen sampling the "local fare."

Opening the front door with a flourish, one arm pointing out, he hustled us from the restaurant. I gave Māko another hug and wished him luck. Ruth smiled at him, and then gave me a smooch before she and Māko walked toward their home.

Roy waved and shuffled back across the paved road to his gas station. The years showed in his gait.

Sarang and I drove along the Hana Highway to the bridge, the easiest and closest link to Hana. Once in town, I squeezed the Mustang, now with the engine revving, into a parking place right in front of Nagasako's *World News Daily* & Office Supplies. The name was an exaggeration, as the paper was local, and a weekly to boot, but typical of the Nagasako family proclivity toward hyperbole. Sarang waited in the car while I went in to drop off the memory card. When I opened the aluminum framed glass door, I smelled printing fluids.

Despite the store's 1980s facade, its products had kept up with the times. Inside, antiquated wood shelves displayed modern digital and video equipment. It was the odd dichotomy of a small town with big bucks. I walked directly to the young man working the counter and waited while he thumbed through what appeared to be him carefully alphabetizing orders. After ignoring me for about a minute, he looked up through his wire-framed glasses and said, "Can I help you?" He made it clear that he hoped the answer would be no.

"I need these images printed right away in the jumbo size." I reached for a processing envelope. "It'll go on the Police's Department account. Should I fill out one of these anyway?"

A confused look crossed his pockmarked face.

"Uh, I'll have to check with Mr. Nagasako." Then he completed his filing before shuffling through the swinging bar doors to the office.

Mr. Nagasako came to the front counter and said, "Why you need charge account?" Peering over his half-glasses, the elderly man inspected me from head to heel. "Don't you have no money?" Nice question from a man wearing a stained button-down shirt tucked into brown polyester bellbottoms.

"Pardon me?" I stuttered.

"Yeah, yeah, yeah," he responded more to the clerk than to me. Then he turned and pushed through the walnut-stained bat-wing doors to the backroom.

"Mr. Nagasako, remember to preserve the chain of custody on this," I called to his back. I knew I had to be a careful customer with this guy. My own experience with the Nagasakos—though years past—still stung me to the core. It was his daughter, Dee Dee Nagasako, Mallory's college roommate, who had run with the Brother Love story and photos. This trip just kept getting better.

He mumbled, "Be done in an hour," and returned to his office. I left with a vain attempt at slamming the front door. Mostly, the bell jangled like crazy. I hoped that Dhong had made the correct decision by having the images printed locally.

I climbed behind the wheel of Buffy and wondered if Mr Nagasako's rudeness was universal or if I rated special animosity. Maybe I was just imagining it. Maybe he hated me. Maybe I was overreacting. So much for the joy of small town living, the simple life and good neighbors. Jerks live in small towns too. They just have more power.

I tried to leave a little rubber in front of the store as I wheeled out. Sarang remained silent. When we pulled into the clinic parking lot, she grabbed her bag and got out. "I'll be right back," she said. Translation: "Wait here."

Watching in my rearview mirror, I waited until Sarang passed through the spinning door before I hopped from the car and entered the facility. The potpourri of medicine and antiseptic—with just a hint of overcooked green beans—assaulted my senses. I spotted my sister just as she turned right at the far end of the hall. Following her, my flip-flops squeaked through empty waiting areas save for the respiratory zone where several seniors sucked on oxygen. I too, turned right and found myself at a suite labeled Lab. Through an open door, I could see Sarang already seated and a tech plunging a needle into her arm. I whirled away from the sight.

Chapter Eleven

I'd seen enough. Sarang was sick. I tried to calm myself. At least she was participating in conventional treatment. Then I remembered her at the springhouse earlier. The hint that she was also treating herself with herbs made me shiver. She could be masking or even inhibiting her treatment—and I doubted that she would tell her doctor. The idea of losing my sister paralyzed me. My entire personality intertwined with my sisters. First, my oldest sister Liebe with breast cancer, now Sarang. What did she have? What would happen if her treatment failed?

I race-walked back to the receptionist at the entrance. I had to find out what was wrong and I wasn't sure Sarang would tell me. She had been an interrogator, first in Iraq, then in Afghanistan. She knew more about keeping and breaking secrets than I could imagine.

"I just dropped my sister off for her treatment. Her name's Sarang Jones. I can't remember her doctor's name, but I was wondering if he's available?" I made lots of eye contact with the woman—begging.

"Oh, let's see, I believe she's seeing Dr. Pease. You wait right here and I'll run see if he's in his office."

That name sure sounded familiar.

In a moment, the nurse was back, signaling me to follow her. Her quick, crisp gait matched her immaculate white slacks. At the last door before an emergency exit, she pointed me to a modest office lined with bookshelves.

Hacking on the computer keyboard was a short man with thick, unruly hair. He stood to greet me, "Hello, I'm Dr. Pease. And you are?" His direct gaze and deep FM-radio voice, almost magically increased his stature as he popped a mint in his mouth.

"Hi, I'm Aloha Jones, Sarang Jones's sister." I swallowed. I needed to be tricky here. "Uh, I just dropped her off for her treatment. And I'm... I'm afraid she might be using some traditional herbs, and, uh, I wanted to make sure they didn't cause problems."

"Well, let's go talk with Sarang and see what she has to say. As you know, I can't share any information with you without her permission."

He guided me through a maze while he chattered about the weather. Across from the lab, he opened an examination room and asked me to make myself comfortable. The examination table, covered with white paper decorated with dancing purple Zebras and some drug name, didn't look too inviting. Instead, I perched on the little rolling stool nearby and listened to murmuring across the hallway. A bin on the wall for needle disposal had a padlock. Ew! Who would steal a used needle?

The door opened. Sarang moved to sit in the one chair in the room, while the doctor leaned against the examination table.

"Sarang has post-traumatic stress disorder." Pease didn't waste any time in dropping the hammer. "She's been having problems coping. It's common with those in her line of work."

He made it sound like she'd stubbed her psychological toe. My heart continued to beat, but I didn't know why. I didn't understand why he was doing all the talking while Sarang remained mute.

"She promised me that when she came to a tipping point that she would call you for help rather than act on her feelings." He stopped to look at Sarang.

"The fires..." she said, "They were the last straw. I'm sorry."

"What do you mean?" I thought I understood the subtext, but I didn't want to believe it.

"I feel numb, Aloha. I can't sleep. I'm so angry. And, I just don't want to deal with anyone or anything. It's all I can do to look normal."

I decided to nod instead of talk. Sometimes the wise choice is listening. I'm trying to acquire the skill.

"It's one of the reasons I asked you to come home," Sarang said. "I didn't want to tell you on the telephone or in an email—and I didn't want you finding out from anyone else." She seemed to shrink as she spoke, the weight of the words showing through her resilient veneer.

"But you've always been able to handle it." I raced toward denial, the first stage of grieving.

"Aloha, what I saw in The Sandbox, what I did. I'm just not able to connect the dots in a way that makes sense." Sarang nodded slightly to the doctor as though dismissing him. He moved to the door.

Confused by his hasty dismissal, I tried to stop him. "Dr. Pease…?"

Sarang held up her hand, signaling me to silence. "He needs to go before I continue," she said. Once the door closed, she honored me with a wry grin. "Remember when I told you about the benefits of plants in healing when you were in high school? Around the same time, we talked about illegal drugs. Well, those two topics are intertwined again."

My eyebrows rose. It couldn't be!

"This morning, you caught me chewing cannabis. For years, people have used dried gravel root for urinary, menstrual, and prostrate treatments. Its scientific name is *Eupatorium purpureum*, but it refers to the root. The whole plant is *Eupatorium cannabium*."

I blinked.

"Well, I think of it as one step removed from Cannabis sativa—I chew it whenever the anxiety is too much." Stated matter-of-factly, it meant that my sister was a human "weed-whacker."

All I could do was stare while my internal voice chanted, "Too much information. Too much information." Peering at the Marine she had been, I saw a hint of a blush. My sister was embarrassed!

"Well, come on. I guess we should get going." I pretended I had just heard the weather forecast—afternoon trade winds, *mauka* showers, and a toking sister.

I hid my surprise at finding out my idol was using dope to fight stress. No wonder the doctor left. He probably knew—and maybe even recommended it in a peripheral manner—but he did not want to know the details of her illegal drug use. Sure, he could have prescribed the pharmaceutical form of the plant, but this was probably Sarang's way of grasping for control in her own treatment.

Smart doctor or bad doctor, I wasn't sure. State law said physicians could legally approve the drug's use, contradicting federal law. From what Snake said, it was a pain for police and judges to separate the wheat from the chaff or the medicinal growers from the recreational users.

Even with the federal and state discrepancies, homegrown was illegal. Was she buying on the street? I didn't like the thought of that at all. Then, I grinned, hoping my sister wasn't "carrying." We still had to drop the dive gear at the police station, and I didn't want a K-9 officer alerting on her.

I absolutely needed to call Snake.

"Nice shots," the clerk at Nagasako's commented when he handed me the prints.

I snatched the images from his hand and pushed my way out the door. How dare he comment! All I wanted to do was drop the images at the police department, call Eddie, and spend the day working with Sarang at the cabin. In fact, I wanted to stick to Sarang like a shadow—at least until my independent sister tired of my intrusion. I'd have to blow off my lunch with Lindy; I knew she'd understand. Besides, it might be better to get away with her in the evening when we could have time to visit.

First stop, the Hana City Hall where the business offices, library, fire department, police department and maintenance garage are all crammed into a huge old warehouse. The company that had owned the land and three-block-long building could never find a suitable buyer and hadn't stayed current on their taxes. Eventually the city took over the property, sold their other properties for big bucks, performed interior remodeling on the gargantuan warehouse, and put "everything under one roof."

It wasn't pretty, but it was smart. What more could you ask for?

Sarang headed to the library while I passed through the main entrance to the police department. A young man wearing a headset gave me directions to find the coroner, then handed me a scribbled note from Lindy, setting up a rendezvous at Pau Hana's later in the evening. Apparently, she too needed to reschedule. The dispatcher then directed me to the door marked Personnel Only. From his workstation, he electronically unlocked the door.

Once inside, I followed his directions to the crime lab, where I could complete my assignment.

A sign posted at the alcove informed visitors to "Press Button For Service." After doing so, a man in disposable scrubs came through the door marked Morgue. Dried blood decorated his pale green paper slacks and shirt. His appearance stopped me cold.

My hands shook as I turned the sealed package of photographs and thumb drive over to him, along with a shot list I'd written earlier identifying each frame. The coroner tossed the package into an "IN" basket as he returned to the autopsy room. This made me blanch.

"Excuse me—" I caught his attention as the door began to close behind him. "Shouldn't that be placed in a secure area? It's evidence."

"Listen, I'm this town's duly elected coroner. This case," he emphasized the word with curled finger-quotes, "is an accident. Period." Then with a smirk, honestly a smirk, he added, "I could tell by the smell of it when I got within ten feet."

My internal alarms began clanging.

"I'm sorry," I said. "I didn't introduce myself properly. I'm Aloha Jones with the Maui Marine Patrol." I didn't mention my status. "You must be Doctor…"

"No. I'm not a doctor," he interrupted. "The coroner is an elected position. It doesn't require medical training." I saw him puff out his chest.

"Then how do you perform autopsies?"

"One of the EMTs does the slicing and dicing. Then they give me a report."

He noticed my glance at the dark spots on his scrubs. "I do the mucking up afterwards and get everything to the labs. I dropped some specimens today and got spattered."

"Have you completed the report on this case already?" Quickly I added, "With your experience, this must be pretty routine." My conscience puked.

He beamed at my appraisal and offered me the file. I flipped through the report, noting that he implemented standard procedures, despite his apparent ineptitude and what seemed like limited training. In the back few pages, I slowly reviewed the photos taken at the onset of the autopsy. The first series included axial and lateral views of the body before disrobing. Mallory's wetsuit had been unzipped to the waist, her bathing suit cut in the same pattern. Three small white discs remained on her chest from the EKG mounts. There was a fourth circular impression above her left breast that was slightly larger than the connector imprints on the skin. Cautiously, I asked where the fourth connector had gone.

"Oh, I figure they pulled it off at the scene," he said, dismissing the anomaly.

I had my own theory but wanted to double-check his logic. "Do they always use four electrode tabs on the EKG?"

"Frankly, I don't have any idea, but I'm not going to chase after those boys about a missing EKG tab. The woman was dead as a post. There's no use wasting their time tracking down a hunk of trash. I could have pronounced her dead without the EKG if I'd gone to the scene but, I wasn't getting out of bed in the middle of the night for a simple drowning."

Throughout his speech, I had refrained from making eye contact with him, knowing that my annoyance would show. I focused instead on the glossy shots of Mallory Deems on the shiny stainless steel table.

I was already creating a search pattern and dive plan in my mind. There was more evidence at the reservoir. I hoped that Lindy would be up for another dive. If not, I would break the rules and go alone. This was too important to drop.

At least he was correct in one aspect of his analysis. Mallory Kila Deems had drowned. Even in the photographs, tiny spot-like hemorrhages were visible on her lungs. The notes on the weights of vital organs made that conclusion clear. The lungs logged in at 700 grams, fully double the weight of normal lungs. Apparently too many of the 300 million microscopic air sacs, or alveoli, had flooded, just like a *taro* patch.

Chapter Twelve

Outside the police station, while waiting for Sarang to finish in the library, I called Snake from my cell phone. Indeed the cell tower was back in business. To maintain a little privacy, I paced in the parking lot as I dialed. I told myself I would keep it cool, no big deal, just friends, as the teenager in my head grabbed the phone and said, "Hey, Baby, want to get lucky?" She was really starting to bug me.

"Sure, just don't let my ex-wife find out." Eddie said, always the king of the witty retort.

I bit. "Well, I heard she understands. Some people might even call her the most even-tempered woman on earth." Maybe it was time to pull the phone away from the teenager in my head. Even I knew she'd gone too far.

"You must be thinking of someone else. My ex has a very hostile, sarcastic, passive-aggressive voice inside her, but she's an amazing diver. In fact, I heard she did a body recovery last night."

The only things pregnant in our relationship are the pauses. Word travels fast.

In the background, I could hear his radio squawk.

"Whatcha doing?" I asked, trying to shift his questioning spotlight off my activities. Snake had wanted to be a cop or an outlaw his whole life. I wanted to be a mermaid or a lighthouse keeper. Seemed we both longed for a certain type of independence, and then we found each other. Then we left each other. We always struggled with the independence thing.

"S-7 at the 10."

"Hunh?" Seven was a dead body. I didn't know what a ten was. It drives me crazy when he does the number thing.

"Lunch break at the fire station." He translated.

"I thought S-7 was a dead body?"

"No, T-7's a body, S-7's lunch. Big difference."

Duh.

He let me off the hook. "Had a vehicle prowl on our rig at the Molokai airport. Perp used a magic rock to break the window." Again, he sounded oh-so-superior.

"I'll bite. What's a magic rock?" I felt like a schoolgirl talking to my boyfriend. If there had been a cord on the cell phone to twirl, I'd be twirling it.

"You slide the porcelain end of a spark plug across the glass and it explodes with the resonance."

"Good to know. Anything else?" I asked, as I logged this piece of trivia into the hard drive in my brain. That meant that something else would get erased. I hoped it was the melody of *It's A Small World*.

"Yeah, had a Russian try to bribe me out of a possession ticket."

"Wow! Are you retiring?"

"I can't be bought for five bucks."

"Dang, I hoped otherwise."

"Only by you, Babe," he paused. "Well, on second thought, I guess not. I'm a one-woman-man, and I've got my sights set on getting back with my ex."

I nearly melted. I'd spent my life waiting for the perfect guy and I was pretty sure, that it wasn't Snake.

"So what else is going on?"

"I took a meth addict to the hospital."

"Details." I'm thinking white guy, mid-thirties, malnourished. Snake surprised me.

"Twenty-seven, female, Hawaiian. What else?"

"What do you mean by that?" I bristled. The racist accusation made me hypersensitive. Not funny. Mr. Perfect has flaws.

"Aloha, Hawaiians have the highest rate of incarceration in the state. In some ways they're lost souls inexorably drawn to booze, dope and abuse." His empathy showed even though his words were harsh.

"Why?"

"They lost their culture. They used to call themselves *kanaka maoli*. It means true human beings. Some basic element of that humanity was lost when they had to give up their historic religion, including chanting and dancing."

"That was a long time ago," I countered, even though I'd started dancing hula to regain my balance as part of my own recovery from an underwater explosives accident while in the Coast Guard. That accident had ended my military career. I love hula. For me it was the ultimate connection to Nature.

While my inner voices began familiar chants, Eddie stayed on topic.

"I'm just trying to remind you that times have changed in the Islands." Then he said, "Be careful. I don't think diving the dam was a good idea."

"Just doing my job, Agent Aquilae." That passive-aggressive voice he mentioned was out.

"Aloha…," Eddie started.

Before he could give me the "be careful" lecture again, I said, "I'm being careful." Then I picked his brain on the medical marijuana laws, but I didn't tell him why. Of course, he didn't ask. He valued his independence and always gave me mine, whether I needed it or not. I felt my heart break. It was suddenly so hard to hang up the phone.

"Oops, gotta go." I heard him cover the phone and say something muffled.

"Anything else?" I tried to keep him on the line a little longer.

"Nope." He said, all cop, no time.

I sighed as I ended the call. This was getting complicated again.

When Sarang came out of the library, we hopped in the car.

"Back to the cabin?"

Sarang just nodded and remained a little mellow if not melancholy as we drove. The dogs greeted us in a manner that made my troubles diminish and we spent the afternoon moving hoses and clearing brush. The fire might have passed, but we didn't know what the winds would do next.

We finished late, and as the sun dropped low, the skies turned from a fabulous glowing orange to purple. It would have been nice to enjoy the one positive result of the fire's wrath. As it was, I barely had time to shower before going to meet Lindy.

My first step into Pau Hana, the local bar with a name that translated to "after work," erased all the pleasure I felt during my afternoon working with Sarang. The place smelled like dry rot, old grease, and cigarettes—I wanted to hold my nose.

Voices fueled with beer erupted over women's loud laughter. Amidst the chatter, I could hear one female sharing the latest antics of her baby-daddy. If there was one phrase, I hated more than any other it was baby-daddy.

A large group sat a table close to the entrance drinking domestic beer and imported wine, while vaping electronic cigars. Gag, gag and triple gag.

Just then, the bartender's fan club erupted with applause—he'd come to the punch line of his best joke. They retreated to their drinks, echoing his words "Follow the yellow-dick toad."

Ugh!

I saw Lindy reading a menu in a booth tucked under a staircase. Seeing me, she rolled her eyes and waved me over. "It's been so long since I've been in a bar that I feel like a dope," Lindy whispered, as I scooted across the torn and worn red vinyl cushion opposite her. "It always seems so great in my memories, but as soon as I sit down, I want to leave."

We grimaced together at our altered perspectives, still remembering the days when Mad Dog 20-20 was our idea of fine wine.

"Do you think they have Boone's Farm on tap?" An involuntary shudder ran up my spine even as I made the joke. I could see Lindy trying to control a heaving response at the memory. This was my way of paying her back for the "must've been love" comment.

"Good thing you were lying next to the sidewalk that night. The storm drain saved me from having to clean up after you."

"Okay, enough on that subject," Lindy retorted. "After all, I am in law enforcement now. I wouldn't want anyone to know my dirty little secrets although I don't mind if they know yours."

We had both managed to maintain an illusion of moderation among our peers, and a modicum of innocence for our parents. Only the poor boys we'd dated knew how bad we could be—but for the most part, they liked bad girls.

Before we could begin catching up, a server took our orders—two Caesar salads and diet Cokes that she delivered immediately. Yay, the salads came with toasted garlic bread! Lettuce was my one concession regarding green food. Who says I'm inflexible?

"I dropped stuff off at the coroner this morning." I let the statement hang while I sipped my soda before the foam overflowed and left a puddle on the chipped laminate table.

"Did you meet Gomer?"

I snorted, a spray of Coke erupting from my nose, as I laughed at his name. "The coroner? Is that really his name?"

"Well, no, it's actually Coroner Gommer, but you can see why we call him Gomer." The obscure reference to Gomer Pyle was a perfect hit. The coroner even spoke with a whiny, southern accent.

"You've probably figured out that he's not qualified to watch an autopsy, let alone lead one." Lindy squeezed her eyes shut as if to erase a mental image of him. "I'm sure you've run into this before."

I shook my head in the negative. I'd never seen such incompetence in my life.

Given Lindy's opinion of the man, I gave her the details of my discussion with him. "When I dropped off the images, he didn't seem to care at all about the chain-of-custody. Then he let me look through the whole file, so I saw the autopsy photographs. There were three white EKG tabs on Mallory's chest. What bothered me was what looked like a contact lividity impression of a fourth. When I looked at the shots taken after they'd removed the wetsuit and the tabs, it wasn't the same size or imprint at all."

I let the information sink in for a moment before I continued. "I bet Mallory was carrying a camera on her dive. I know that embossed skin look. I used to see it in the mirror."

Still Lindy mugged a quizzical look. I continued with my theory after a long pull from my drink. "Most underwater photographers keep their lens cap tucked inside their wetsuit. The shape I saw in the photo looked like that. Gommer said he listed all the items brought in with the body on the autopsy report. No lens cap was included. When I asked him if there are any further dives scheduled, he laughed."

I paused while the server refilled our waters. Lindy still looked puzzled.

"I want to do the dive again. If we can find her camera, it will tell us what she was doing out there." I had slipped in the "we" for Lindy's sake. It was only prudent that we pursue this as a team, since it seemed no one else was thinking along these lines.

"Are you sure?" Lindy said. "I mean, I'm in, but we need to be careful. I think you're right to check on this. If we find anything, will you show Dhong?"

Weird question, but I blew it off. I had missed Lindy. I just knew we would find a camera. What I didn't know was what the images would reveal.

We continued to discuss the mission and created a clear set of objectives. Then we caught up on life in general. Lindy, who had married the day after high school graduation and divorced a year later, said she had been dating a local guy for a couple months. According to her, their relationship was in the "Let's move in together and see how it goes and call it engaged" stage. Lindy didn't mention his name and I allowed her that privacy—for now.

Despite our general gossiping, I didn't mention the problems I saw in the police department. Nor was I ready to share the information about Sarang's illness and self-medicating, since I was still processing my own feelings after my sister and I had spent the entire afternoon talking about her treatment.

With Sarang's illness bearing down on my soul, I was feeling helpless and alone. When I feel this way, it's like looking through a scratched camera lens. There are general shapes, but no details.

Before I could broach a new subject with Lindy, I heard angry male voices at the bar. One shouted, "You killed her!" In a glance, I recognized my long lost ex-boyfriend, Nate Deems, standing next to the bar. Instead of the dark curly locks he'd once boasted, he had transitioned to the totally shaved look with the obligatory soul patch. He held Kāne Nooner, Kū's moon-faced brother, by his tank top straps. Then he pushed the drunken man off his bar stool.

Lindy reached behind her back to check for her gun before pulling her phone from her purse. She punched in 9-1-1 and spoke rapidly to the dispatcher, requesting an officer at Pau Hana. She then calmly walked to where the two men were poking, shoving and growling at each other like two dogs trying to mark the same rock.

"Nate." Lindy stepped between them. "Kāne."

"Hey, Lindy, don't worry. We were just leaving," Nate said, grabbing Kāne by the arm.

"I'm not going anywhere with you, man!" Kāne pushed his palm flat against Nate's chest, and then turned away. Bad choice.

Again, Nate reached for Kāne. This time, Kāne lashed out with a blind swing, connecting with the side of Lindy's head, nearly knocking her down.

Someone was going to finish the evening in jail.

Straightening quickly, Lindy lost all patience. "Okay, you two, I have back-up on the way. Outside!" She put an arm bar hold on Nate and merely gestured to Kāne. "Let's go." As she maneuvered them to the door, looking like a miniature mom with errant teenagers, she motioned me to follow.

Once out in the looming dusk, Lindy told each of the men to place their hands on her car while she patted them down for weapons. Neither man carried a gun, though each had a tool on his belt that combined a set of pliers, a ruler, a screwdriver, a file, an awl and a can opener, all neatly tucked into a leather case. It seemed like this was the modern version of the childhood Swiss Army knife, since nearly every guy I knew had one. Secretly, I suspected that they were waiting to add a decoder ring to complete the kit.

"Okay, guys, let's talk about this. If you can settle it before the other officer gets here, maybe you can avoid spending the night in jail."

Huh?

Despite being out of uniform and off-duty, both guys had to know if you hit a cop, you go to jail. Who was she trying to kid?

Kāne spoke first, looking at Lindy and ignoring Deems. "I don't know what this dude wants with me. I think he's pissed that I'm Hawaiian." Kāne *would* make this a race-related incident. He had always been on the edge of the law, and now found plenty of followers for his pet theories on government conspiracies against native peoples. For special emphasis, he added a sad, moping expression to his face, as if to coax Lindy to take his side based on their common skin tone.

Geez, and I was called racist?

"Uh, right," Lindy said. Then, she turned to Nate. "What's the scoop?" She looked like she was acting the part of a cop rather than being a cop. What was that all about? Sometimes I had felt that way in my former life, mostly when I had a victim's family watching me set up gear, when I knew I'd be bringing their loved one out dead, not alive. Their hope broke my heart. I had to act detached, professional and without emotion.

"It's private." Nate's eyes were blood-shot and lifeless, his skin, though deeply tanned, seemed wan and puffy. His grief had aged him.

"Fine. I'll wait here with you guys until the patrol car comes." Lindy made it clear she didn't care how they resolved their problem, or even if they simply left each other alone. She seemed comfortable to wait it out with them.

Finally, Nate noticed me. "Aloha, how long you home for?"

There it was again, the reference to home, this time even more poignant, since it came from the man responsible for my departure. In all fairness, I knew it had been my decision, but I couldn't look him in the eye. It caused him to step back. A slap in the face may have been less painful. Still, this man had just lost his wife.

"Nate, I'm so sorry about Mallory." I said, sincere in my sympathy for him, despite my antipathy for his deceased wife.

"I don't know what to do." Struggling for words, Nate simply spoke the truth. Kāne snorted at Nate's comment. Lost in our own reunion, we'd forgotten our audience.

Nate took a step toward Kāne. "Listen pal, what was my wife was doing diving at the dam? You were with her. Why'd you take her diving? Why'd you let her die?" Nate's voice had risen from a choked whisper to a shout.

"Up yours. I wasn't with her. I don't know what she was doing, but I do know that she wasn't your wife—or should I say, you weren't much of a husband." Kāne pushed the words out with his chest, resembling a bantam-rooster crowing his diminutive superiority. Lindy again stepped between the men.

"Aloha, could you take Nate to your car and wait there while I talk to Kāne?" Lindy asked, knowing that she was calling in favors not yet earned. I empathized with her. I could tell she, too, felt sorry for Nate—and even Kāne—though for no apparent reason.

Nothing good would come of this confrontation, yet my loyalty to her came before my opinion. She needed to separate the men and knew I could handle myself. If anyone should be worried, it was Nate.

"Okay," I said, and led Nate away.

"Is this your car?" Nate eyed the vintage Mustang as though he was a hunter and it was a six-point buck. "You must be doing well, Aloha."

"Uh...." I stumbled for an answer. It was a gift from my parents, but originally had been Snake's toy. Should I say it belonged to my ex-husband?

Nate slid onto the black leather seat and caressed the dash's wooden inlay. "What I wouldn't give...," he murmured.

It just made me love the car more. "Her name's Buffy," I blurted.

He didn't seem to hear me, so I focused on controlling my feelings and the situation at hand. This was not how I'd envisioned my reunion with Nate. Even more amazing was that it simply did not matter anymore what he thought of me.

He still had the tall, dark and dangerous complexion that had first attracted me, even though I'd always had a weakness for the fair-haired golden-boys, too. His frame had changed to that of an active adult male versus the lanky kid I'd known.

Okay, whom was I kidding? I liked 'em blonde, brown-haired and even bald. I smiled thinking of my top ten favorite men. It included a variety of ages and styles from Sam Elliott to Pitbull to Owen Wilson. I dig diversity if for nothing more than a spectator sport.

Nate dragged me back from my happy fantasy world. "Sorry to pull you into this," he said, watching Kāne's interrogation. "I don't know why he called me here."

Huh, from my viewpoint it seemed like Nate had been looking, for Kāne, not visa versa.

"No need to apologize Nate. But resolve whatever *this* is in a non-violent manner." It felt good to be the responsible one. The multiple personalities that usually kidney-punched and bickered inside my head did a big high five.

Then I switched gears. "I helped recover Mallory's body last night. I thought you'd be there." No question asked, only implied. I waited patiently, knowing that most people had the uncontrollable urge to fill in a quiet void.

"I couldn't handle seeing her like that," he said as he looked away. A tear leaked from eye and bled down to his chin. "When Missy died, I was there, but I didn't want to remember Mallory as a corpse."

I waited for him to continue.

"I stayed at the house while Mallory's mom did the identification." Without missing a beat, he added, "She's probably better at that sort of thing than I am anyway."

A tingle ran up my spine. How could anyone be good at body identification? Again, I questioned without questions. "That's an interesting thing to say."

Nate seemed to compose himself, again apologizing. "Sorry, I shouldn't have said that. I meant that she's older, more used to death, I guess." In near meter, he stroked the splotch of manicured hair just below his lip, as he slowly spoke the words.

Bingo! My internal lie detector clanged with abandon. Score one for me! I wished I'd known more about body language in my youth. Maybe I would have spotted this man's little quirks sooner. You would have thought his complete lack of a backbone would have been obvious.

"I heard you and Mallory had a daughter." As long as I had him in tears, I might as well continue. I saw him swallow hard, his Adam's apple far more prominent than I'd remembered.

"We named her Melissa, but called her Missy. She was born the year after you left town." Somehow, he made it sound like I'd dumped him. "She had leukemia."

I kept him talking with comments, not questions. "That must have been unbearable." I well understood how impotent it felt to love someone with cancer after the battle my sister Liebe had just won. What I did not quite comprehend was how Nate became a father.

"It was tough for Mallory while Missy was sick. I spent time with her in the hospital and then took care of her at home. It was hardest for me when she died. Deep down, I knew it could happen—but it looked like she was getting better. I would have taken her place. I prayed hundreds of times before, and since, that God would take me instead."

Yeah, I'd kind of prayed the same for him, but that's another story. One I wasn't proud to admit. Nate held his head up, his face to the window, his words familiar from multiple telling.

Outside Lindy finished questioning Kāne while Nate sat with me in my car. It was nearly fifteen minutes before the officer-on-duty left Pau Hana's pot-holed parking lot with Kāne in the back of his cruiser. I almost felt bad for him. Nothing like a night in jail to sober you up.

I should have felt guilty for pulling painful memories from Nate's wounded soul. I didn't. There were still too many unanswered questions. Too bad Lindy was walking toward us. Using my least confrontational demeanor and tone, I kicked him in his emotional nuts. "Then you must have been thrilled that Mallory was pregnant again."

He opened the car door and threw up.

Oh yeah, I'm smooth.

Chapter Thirteen

"Seems like that went well," Lindy observed, once I bailed out of my car and Nate climbed into his SUV. Maybe I needed to get one of those. The aging Mustang was too small for heartfelt discussions, interrogations and confessions.

First, I needed to settle the history with my former best friend.

"Lindy, I'm really sorry I didn't keep in touch better. I think of you all the time—and I just assumed you'd always be here for me—but please don't ever stick me in a car with my ex-boyfriend, who lost his wife, nearly got into a fight and could be a suspect in a homicide. Geez, why didn't you just shoot me when I drove into town?"

A sparkle in my eye betrayed the gruff talk and sullen expression that accompanied the comment.

Lindy, using tactics learned in the academy, remained silent, waiting for me to fill in the void. In my career, I had learned the same technique. I simply maintained eye contact without saying a word. The stare-down was like taking a jump back in time to childhood. Stare-downs were quite the skill then, and we had both been masters. Ever so slowly, the twinkles grew to grins and then the inevitable eye rolling. Still no words. Finally, Lindy scrawled one word on my notebook and showed it to me. "Truce."

I nodded in agreement and said, "Nate said some pretty strange stuff. Maybe I've been gone too long. Everything seemed wrong."

Lindy was not one to talk in circles. "What'd he say?"

I recounted my conversation with Nate, then added, "It seemed like he was lying half the time. I thought I knew him so well, but I don't." I looked at my hands—especially the finger that I'd once thought would wear his ring.

"I mean, I knew the basic stuff about him and his family, but I didn't know much about him as a person."

"Sounds like Fate stepped in when Brother died," Lindy said as she turned to go back to the restaurant. I could see her expression reflected in the window. If I had to guess, I'd have said it held animosity. So much for accurate mirror images.

"She has a sick sense of humor, and justice," I said, referring to Fate. "Now we need to figure out if she stepped in for Mallory—or if she had help." I had no answer. Lindy didn't press. She knew me well—the only time I'd run away was after Brother's death. The rest of my life I'd been a person that ran toward danger, if not conflict. For the time being, she allowed me to avoid answering. I changed the subject to our return trip to the dam. We planned to dive for the underwater camera the following morning.

After leaving Lindy, I drove the back roads to the cabin. They remained deserted. When I pulled into Sarang's driveway, the various disasters seemed invisible. The true divided-light windows of the old plantation house created a Norman Rockwell scene. Wharf jumped up from his position on the porch and ran to my car, peering in the window as he trotted up the driveway alongside it. I regretted not having spent more time with him. I felt pulled in too many directions since my return. At least I didn't have much time to dwell on my own feelings. It seemed I was the only one holding onto the past. No one else seemed to give a rip, except maybe Haspin, which was weird considering he wasn't a part of it.

Bringing Wharf inside the cabin with me, I smiled at Sarang curled up on the couch with a book. Stinger held down the carpet at her feet. I settled into a well-worn glider with Wharf resting his head on the wooden arm, his golden-brown eyes locked on mine in adoring wonder.

"What's the word on the fire?" I asked.

"I heard that a few pockets of jungle are smoldering on the surrounding ridges, but the threat of further firestorms is unlikely now."

Sarang seemed nervous even though one threat was gone. Then she added, "They're keeping enough firefighters on hand to make the press conference look good tomorrow."

She frowned at the thought of the looming media spectacle. "That Hunt Goldswaithe thought he could beat us out of the water in court. Now that he's with the Environmental Protection Agency, he probably thinks he can hold out on federal aid for the fires."

"What do you mean? What did he have to do with water rights? I didn't even know he was from Hawai'i until he showed up as the head of EPA. I always assumed he was a D.C. wonk, milking the taxpayers for his wage." I shared the region's intrinsic distrust of the powers-that-be on the Mainland.

"They tried to reach a negotiated settlement before it went to court. Goldswaithe advised the state to fight," Sarang explained as she held one finger in her book to hold her place. "That's when Kāwika began representing the community, separate from the other towns."

Up until the mention of Kāwika, I assumed this was my sister's standard diatribe against the government, which was kind of funny for a Marine, but true. Now she had my full attention.

"The *taro*'s water need was so small compared to the town that it was gobbled up in the early negotiations. Kāwika filed a separate suit for us. Thanks to him, we have a six-square-mile lake."

This history was remotely familiar. I knew Kāwika was a local hero and that the town had done well in a court settlement. However, I wasn't clear on Goldwaithe's reasons for coming to the community. On the other hand, why was it such a big deal?

"Seems like Goldswaithe did everyone a favor by being incompetent." I said.

"But in the process he antagonized folks around here more than necessary. He spoke down to us, especially the Hawaiians. He insinuated they were drunks by nature, and lazy by nurture. He wasn't welcome here then, and he's not welcome here now. Those firefighters you saw this morning at Ruth's are the local guys. They take pride in their heritage and training. They don't want to stand on the same earth as Goldswaithe, let alone next to him onstage."

I remembered the hostility and anger at Māko's, but I still didn't understand why he caused such antagonism in the Hawaiian community.

It didn't matter though. I wouldn't be around to witness the press statement. "Lindy and I are diving again tomorrow. I think we missed something the other night." I tried to sound nonchalant, casually stroking Wharf's ears, not looking at Sarang as I spoke, and using a low, even tone of voice.

To an outside observer, my deception worked, as my sister's only response was "No problem." I, however, knew that her coded response really meant, "huge problem."

"What do you mean, 'No problem'?" I betrayed my discomfort with the question.

"Just that. It's no problem that you are going diving tomorrow."

"Yeah, right. If it were really no problem, you wouldn't have said, 'No problem.'"

"Aloha, you're getting paranoid. I really meant no problem. Maybe you have a guilty conscience."

Ouch. That barbed arrow pierced the truth like a dart on in the bull's-eye. Indeed, I was feeling guilt about not visiting more with my sister. Sarang was such a straight shooter that I knew the best way to assess her actual feelings was simple directness.

"I guess you're right. I am feeling guilty. I don't feel like I'm helping you with the fire, with the stress, with anything. So far, I used the cabin as a hotel one night while I worked. I followed you into a private meeting with your physician. I have neither kept watch nor offered any assistance." I rubbed my fingers through Wharf's luxurious coat. "Yep, I feel guilty."

"Don't," Sarang sighed. "Having you here is all I ever wanted or needed. I've missed you terribly. Don't beat yourself up over things you can't control. You came when I called. Who could have known that you'd have to work? The fire moved on. I've had months to deal with my issues. I realize that having you here won't solve them. I'll do everything the doctor says, while I continue to treat myself naturally. Enjoy your time with a clear heart. That's all I ask of you." Sarang scratched Stinger's rump at that perennially itchy spot where her tail rests.

"Uh, have you told Ike and Eve?" I asked, hoping my parents would handle the news in a manner that didn't involve me.

The ringing phone interrupted the moment.

"It's Lindy." I said, as I looked at the caller ID.

"Did you read the paper yet?" Lindy said in an excited voice.

"No, what's in it?" I had bigger fish to fry at the moment.

"Mallory made the front page, a lovely portrait of her underwater." Lindy's voice reeked of sarcasm.

"What idiot took that? From inside the viewing room? Who's listed on the photo credit?"

Lindy didn't answer.

"Hey, Lindy..." I got up and moved to the porch.

"Aloha, you have the photo credit. It says your name." She paused for a moment.

The Nagasakos used one of my photos! My heart raced. What was their beef? How did this happen to me? How would I ever rectify their gross misconduct? These thoughts circulated in my head while Lindy continued speaking. Add this to the racial discrimination accusation and my career in the Islands was over.

By the time I hung up the phone, Sarang had gone to bed. I called the paper and listened to a recorded message. I didn't leave my name. Instead, I hung up the phone and wept. With Wharf on the floor next to me, I fell asleep on the couch clutching a wad of tissue.

As was usual, when I was working on an investigation, the deceased's last moments filled my subconscious. In my often, terrifying dreams, I would recall details I'd missed—like watching a movie in slow motion. My *kumu hula*—what we called our teacher—had told me that dreams are real, whether daydreams or experienced when asleep. The movies they play in our heads are no different from the reality of life as they influence our emotions and actions. This dream proved her correct.

Skinny Mallory, I thought. She had to be cold during her dive. Her wetsuit was too large. Diving alone had to give her a severe adrenaline rush. Was she scared? My body shivered and tensed as I dreamed. She couldn't see the bottom of the reservoir. She didn't have a compass. How did she plan to find her photo subject? What did she want to shoot?

When did panic set in? Her weight belt was missing, so were both fins. She had to have pulled the quick release on the belt, hoping to buoy to the surface. I assumed the fins went downstream in the current.

The full force of the water caught her slight frame. The bars bruised her legs when she tumbled through the concrete tube trying to catch something—anything. Was she alive when she reached the viewing window? Oh, for a "magic rock" on the one-inch thick, clear viewing panels between life and death. Not that it would have flooded the room and incapacitated the dam. Even my screwy subconscious threw out ludicrous thoughts.

Had someone been in the viewing room, they would not have heard her feeble taps. Instead, they would have witnessed a horrifying sight as

Mallory gasped her last breath. No doubt, she screamed as she frantically kicked and clawed at the window. Finally, in her dying act, she would have aspirated enough water to render herself unconscious.

Whom did she think of then? Was it Nate, Missy, her mother, maybe Kāne?

The ending of the dream was always the same—death by drowning. What in the world, was Mallory doing diving at the dam with a camera?

Tomorrow I'd find out.

On my second sojourn to the reservoir the following morning, it looked different. Daylight and clearing skies lent color and life that had been missing in the dark. Crime scene tape littered the parking lot.

While I waited for Lindy, I searched the area surrounding the space where Mallory had parked, including the boat ramp where she had presumably entered the water. That's where I found the lens cap.

Despite being alone, I felt the community peering over my shoulder. From the tire tracks, it looked like half the town had visited the scene. I realized further searching was probably futile since the number of different and overlapping footprints in the dust validated the popularity of the site. In the fifteen minutes, I spent waiting for Lindy to join me I gained little insight on the case.

Lindy arrived in her patrol car, wearing shorts and a tank top over a one-piece swimsuit. Her short dark hair pulled back into the world's smallest ponytail made her look about nineteen.

"Morning," Lindy muttered. "Did you figure out why they used your shot?"

"No. By the time I called the paper last night, no one answered. This morning the editor was miraculously out of the office."

"You don't sound like you believe them."

I rolled my eyes. "Once we're done here, I'll sort this out in person. It's tougher to screen visitors than to screen calls. If I go there, someone will have to deal with me."

I handed Lindy the lens cap. She rewarded me with an enthusiastic "Wow!" Then said, "Guess we don't need to dive now."

"Yeah we do," I said. "We have to find the camera. Come on." My words brought us back to the task. Together we looked across the water to where it backed up to the dam. It was a formidable structure.

We suited up without preamble and our pre-dive check went without a hitch.

"So, shall we start here at the ramp and work our way out along the bottom?" Lindy asked.

"We need to dive our deepest dive first. This could take several tries. If we have to get the tanks refilled, that profile will give us a good surface interval."

Lindy shivered.

"Are you nervous about the depth of the dive?"

"I just thought we could go in gradually." Lindy appeared distracted. I attributed it to her having forgotten the rule about diving the deepest profile first. I let it slide so as not to fluster her further.

To complete our task successfully, we brought string and spikes to mark each pass. With a depth of ninety feet for the first target zone, we had approximately fifteen minutes of bottom time available. Once we surveyed the deeper areas, we would take successive dives at shallower depths with longer bottom times. The likelihood of the camera being lost early in the dive was remote. I reasoned that Mallory would have aborted her dive if she had dropped it early.

"Don't worry," I said, "I'm sure it'll be calm and cool down there today." We needed good conditions; otherwise, it would take us days, maybe weeks, to search the bottom.

I remembered the story of the first public safety dive team in Canada that spent three months looking for a missing gun thrown from a quarter-mile long bridge into water over a hundred feet deep. Their tenacity resulted in a conviction. I hoped that mine would do the same. Then I wondered: When had I begun to think of this as a crime?

Chapter Fourteen

The best thing we had going for us was the lack of bottom grasses and debris along the dam's base. This allowed us to use a larger grid, defined by the added illumination from our underwater lights.

As I got ready, the direct morning sun caused sweat to bead on my forehead. When we moved to the water's edge, my swimsuit worked its way into a powerful wedgie. Talk about distracting.

Again, Wharf packed the heaviest gear right to the shore. I wasn't worried about him. Those who had watched him previously told me that his attention remained focused on my bubble exhalations. Wharf seemed better qualified at diver supervision than some dive boat captains I've worked with.

The body heat generated before the dive made the water seem cool. The thin neoprene wetsuit insulated my body once the layer of water against my skin had warmed. I walked into deeper water and spit in my mask. Waist-deep, I stopped and pulled on my fins, tightening the straps behind my Achilles tendon. Lindy did the same.

We conserved our compressed air by using our snorkels to swim to the search area.

As we submerged, the underwater pressure gradually increased. I saw Lindy pinch her nose while trying to press air through it. Having stretched my Eustachian tubes through years of diving, I merely had to "jack my jaw" to achieve the same effect. Each time I cleared, the sounds of the turbines grew louder, the transmission capabilities of the water amplifying the noise.

In less than two minutes, we made contact with the dam's concrete retaining wall. Without having seen the structure's blueprints, one wouldn't know that it was thirty feet thick, front to back, in this location. Using the wall as our constant, with a pin pounded into the adjacent sediment, we began our search, surveying a width of twenty feet.

In fifteen minutes, our air gauges read 600 psi. We slowly ascended to ten feet for a safety stop, allowing our bodies to off-gas the deadly buildup of nitrogen that causes decompression sickness. With little more than 100 psi in our tanks, we surfaced and kicked to the shore where Wharf lay in the sun.

Lindy and I spent our prescribed surface interval drinking water and laying in the sun quietly gathering energy for a second dive. With eyes shut and the dot of light from the sun penetrating my lids, the sound of Wharf bustling to the water's edge caused me to lift my head. As I raised one hand in a salute above my eyes, I tried to see what had caught his attention. Across the river, a pickup truck had pulled into the shaded parking lot adjacent to the boat ramp. On this side, my car was somewhat camouflaged by the brush surrounding the parking lot. Buffy's matte black finish offered little reflection. With our bodies prone and the sun behind him, the driver couldn't see us. Probably someone on lunch break, seeking solitude, I decided. Then I saw the driver unload dive gear from the back of his rig and head to the shore.

"Lindy, look, there's someone diving on the other side." I nudged her with my arm.

"That's weird." She didn't even open her eyes.

"Yeah," I nudged her again. "Who else dives here?"

"Who cares?"

"I do." I grabbed my second tank and set up my gear. Lindy followed suit, but with far less sense of urgency than I felt. In minutes, we were back in the water sixty feet below the surface.

We had a limited safe bottom time available at this depth. Finding the camera was our priority, but I also hoped to identify the other diver. We got lucky on one, if not the other. Shortly after resuming our original pattern, I found the camera lying on the soft bottom. It was a Nikonos 3 underwater model, its black body barely distinguishable from the surrounding muck.

I shot several frames of the location with my camera, using Lindy and the survey strings as reference points. I noted their coordinates on my slate then picked up Mallory's camera housing by its strap.

With mere minutes left on our dive, we gathered our markers. After another safety stop, we inflated our buoyancy compensating vests, and switching to snorkels, swam to the beach.

As we slogged up the boat ramp, I looked across the reservoir and observed the other diver on the surface. Apparently, he had made a dive with a profile shallower than we had completed. No wonder our paths had not intersected. Someone would have to be crazy to do the dangerous and illegal dive within the restricted zone behind the dam. Crazy—or incredibly motivated.

"Quick! Put your gear in my rig." I was in motion as I spoke. I don't believe in coincidence. Lindy lagged several steps behind me.

"Let's use your car to cross the dam." I urged her along.

"I'll just radio it in." Lindy paused in the front seat of her car, the door still open while she reached for the mic.

"Come on, we need to see what's going on." I pulsated with impatience. "Don't tell me this department has you completely whipped." The not-so-subtle peer pressure worked. Still in wetsuits, we piled into her car. Wharf sat in back. He looked embarrassed to be behind the cage. Lindy slammed her door and idled the car to the gate accessing the dam.

Plant security consisted of a remote video camera and a button with a sign above it that read: "PRESS TO OPEN GATE. ALL DELIVERIES

MUST SIGN IN AT MAIN OFFICE."

Pressing the button, Lindy inched the patrol car toward an overall clad technician crossing the compound. After she honked, he walked to her window and pulled tiny orange foam earplugs from his ears. Safety glasses with side shields hid his eyes and a bright yellow hardhat covered his hair.

"Hi, I'm Officer Somers. I need to get to the other side of the dam. How do I get the gates opened?" She didn't need to flash a badge. Driving a patrol car seemed enough motivation.

"Here, I'll open it for you." He turned and walked to the locked gate. After scrolling through a combination releasing the lock, he grabbed the gate and leaned against it, pushing the chain-link barrier back into a pocket. As soon as we drove through, he closed the fence. With this short cut, we reduced the normal half-hour trek from one side of the lake to the other on county and plantation roads to less than a minute.

On the other side was another push-button primary access gate, which opened automatically with the pressure of a finger. Looking at me, Lindy smiled and shrugged at the apparent lack of security. Was there anything in particular to protect? After all, it was not as if someone would break in to hook up an I-pad or a Prius to steal some power.

The road on the opposite side of the dam was like new. Federal funds periodically flowed for housing, roads and community centers. They were scarce for on-the-job training, drug rehab centers and daycare. The issue continued to be hardware versus software—staggering support statistics versus harsh reality.

Ignorance, until recently, had held me at bay regarding the reason for these funding peccadilloes of promised food, shelter and basic life needs. The concepts of sovereignty and provision were the only reasons the early leaders signed the documents. That and the guns held to their heads, figuratively if not always literally.

At the boat launch, the vehicle we had seen was gone. The only evidence remaining of the mystery diver's presence a trail of water to the parking space nearest the ramp.

"No point in trying to find him now," Lindy said. "Too many roads he could've taken." She turned the cruiser around and again pulled up to the electronic gate at the dam.

"I suppose you're right." The disappointment at not identifying the mystery diver echoed in my voice.

As soon as we got to the other side, she said, "I'll call you later about carpooling to the funeral." The dispatcher called out her number and relayed information. "Sounds like I need to get to work. I'll see you later." She left in a churn of gravel and dust.

The drive back down to Hana gave me time to consider my planned confrontation at the newspaper. My boss, Babs, always told me not to go to war with anyone who buys ink by the barrel. As usual, I ignored her wisdom.

Within a few minutes, I had parked in front of the refurbished mill shack that housed the little press. Inside, the newspaper staff was feverishly stuffing grocery inserts into the latest issue, and most had their backs to the door. Two young men faced the entrance, but they were too deep in conversation to greet me.

While I waited for assistance, I looked through the most recent issue. The newspaper's masthead gave me some answers that helped me formulate a strategy. I walked through the low, bat-wing door and headed directly to the nearest office, where an elderly woman was speaking on the telephone. I put a copy of the photo on her desk.

The woman ended her telephone conversation abruptly. Without asking me to sit she said, "You need to fill out a 1099 for us, and then we'll cut you a check." Almost as an afterthought she said, "Nice shot." After handing me the form, she punched the keypad of her phone, dismissing me with her actions.

"I wanted to make sure you knew my rates." I watched her exhale the way I do when the surfer kids stop in my office at Lahaina Harbor and interrupt me doing something important. She pulled off her glasses, rubbed her eyes with a nasty looking handkerchief, and said, "What the hell are you talking about? We have a standard scale. Don't try that crap with me, Missy."

"Mrs. Nagasako, you used a photograph of mine that I shot during a police investigation—and you did it without my consent. In fact, you used a photograph taken from the chain-of-evidence. I don't know what kind of a rag you're running here, but unless you want to make your payment to me after going to court, I suggest you cut me a check for $1,000 right now. Then we'll walk together to your bank and cash it. Oh, and by the way, don't call me Missy."

The woman blustered and pulled a faded green check register from her top drawer. On it, she scrawled the requisite information. She wrote the check on an account from the bank across the street from the newspaper office. She didn't speak as we walked to the bank, nor at any time during the transaction. She just went along with my blackmail.

With a thousand dollars in my pocket, I wrote a brief review of the circumstances relating to the transaction; signed and dated the missive, then had Mrs. Nagasako do the same.

The Nagasakos were a classic example of the old saw about fruit falling close to the tree—good or bad. For a moment, I wondered where their witchy daughter, Dee Dee, had eventually landed her broom. I didn't realize I'd find the answer to that question from Nate.

Chapter Fifteen

At the city hall, I parked in the last space marked VISITOR. Gathering my purse and the camera, I locked my car and walked across the blistering pavement to the entrance. I could almost see the heat waves radiating into the air. As I placed my hand on the warm door handle, I remembered my notebook and dive slate still in the car. I stomped one foot and headed back to where I had parked.

On the way, I noticed a truck with a dive flag decal in the back window. The rear fender showed a new dent and the bumper folded up enough that the license was barely visible. The truck was cherry-red like the pickup Lindy and I had seen on the other side of the dam. I retrieved my notebook and jotted down the plate number, hoping to get someone inside to run an ownership search on the state vehicle database.

Inside the old warehouse, I headed straight to the police department. After asking to speak to Hana's only detective, and one of my least favorite people, Haspin, I paced in circles around the perimeter of the reception area. Sequential photographs of past and present chiefs lined the walls. Each officer was in uniform. Some scowled. Others grinned. I wondered how long Chief Dhong would stay. According to the unfinished plaque under his name, he had been on the job for only one term.

Before I could muse further, Haspin appeared and motioned me into his office. The title 'Detective' prominently displayed on his door. It looked like he had made the sign himself using rub-on letters. Nice.

He extended his hand. "Aloha, right? I'm Detective Haspin."

"Hi, Haspin. Nice to see you again." That let him know that I knew him already and I didn't care if he was *Chief* Haspin. I'd still call him Haspin and idly wondered why Kū had called him Dog at the roadblock when I arrive in town.

Just then a siren shrieked and I about jumped out of my skin. "What the ... ." I sputtered.

"Policy," he boasted. "We do it every time a patrol unit leaves the building."

"Why?" I fanned my face with my hand trying to calm my pulse.

"The jail's in here too. It reminds all those guys that we're here and to think about us." He beamed.

Gee, I wonder whose idea that was.

"Uh, well, right—Mrs. Jones. It says here on this message that you have something else belonging to our drowning victim." He was now seated and rifling through the messages and reports on his desk. He never looked directly at me. Finding the small white slip of paper, he said. "Yeah, it says right here that you'd drop off the victim's belongings. Now, why didn't you just give them to her family?"

Either this guy was as stupid as a rock or—more stupid than a rock. There didn't seem to be any explanation for his lack of interest in actual evidence.

"I did another dive at the dam and found the victim's underwater camera. It might help you discover the reason for her dive."

I remained standing, even though I knew it put me in a defensive position. It's no accident that judges remain seated.

"Well, that's pretty interesting since everyone we've talked to said she was a beginner. I doubt that she'd try to take pictures, too."

"Either you can take this into evidence and develop the film or I can keep it and submit it as part of my report. Which would you prefer?"

He didn't take long to puzzle out his answer. "Give me the camera. I'll take care of it." Now he was anxious for the prize.

"I'll need an evidence receipt from you. That shouldn't be a problem, should it?" His face reddened. Using his telephone intercom system, he requested a receipt book from the front desk.

"By the way, we can't pay you for the second dive," he said, trying to dissuade me from more involvement. In case I didn't get it, he added, "We don't need your help."

"Is that a directive from Chief Dhong?"

By this time, Haspin was fidgeting behind his desk. Maybe he had to use the bathroom.

"The chief and I haven't discussed your involvement. It's just department policy. We handle our own investigations. This is an accident involving a family that's had more than its share of tragedies."

I crossed my arms and gave him the raised eyebrow look. The one that says, "Yeah, right."

Haspin continued despite my look. "Don't push this into their faces. They're grieving. Leave them alone. Just back off." He dismissed me by lifting his telephone receiver.

Was this my cue to leave? I might respond better if people gave me the equivalent of a doggie biscuit when I did what they wanted, or at least a Nilla wafer. It worked for Wharf. As it was, I didn't want to leave, but had no reason to stay and hassle him further. Too bad, I was starting to have fun.

"Okay, I can tell you're busy. I'll probably see you at the funeral, huh?" A pained expression settled on his face. He really should have offered me a treat if he wanted my obedience.

I dropped the camera at the front desk. Rather than asking the dispatcher to run the identification on the little red pick-up's plates, I tried another tack. "I'm embarrassed to ask this, but I noticed that someone had written a pretty foul comment on that red Ford Ranger outside. Any idea who it belongs to? I can wipe it off on my way out but I don't want to get the owner mad."

"Oh, sh—." She stopped mid-word. "That's my boyfriend's. He's constantly telling my kids not to write on the windows, so of course, they do. They're not wild about him moving in with us, and he's not wild about dealing with a bunch of white kids."

The harried redhead took out her ear bud. She made me think of Sarang. She says that redheads scare her. Clowns too. This gal's hair and makeup combined would have freaked my sister out completely.

With leaking eyes and her mascara beginning to run, she looked up at me. "Could you wipe it off for me? Lone's supposed to drop off my car any minute and take his truck to work. He doesn't need this too."

She pulled a wad of tissues from a box on her desk and passed some to me. She used another one to dab away her streaking eyeliner.

"His name is Lone?" I asked.

"Well it's really Lono. Lono Nooner. I guess Lone Nooner sounds funny. It sounds like he has a "nooner" by himself, if you know what "nooner" means?"

She didn't wait for an answer. Grabbing another handful of tissues, she honked her nose. Sans the squirting flower, the clown image was now complete. "Please—"

"Sure," I said. "I didn't mean to upset you. I just thought someone ought to know." I couldn't believe my good luck. I'd wipe the window down, even though there was nothing written on it.

It was time to catch up with the Nooners.

"What do you mean you want to know everything about him? He's already going with someone and he's not your type," Sarang said.

"What do you mean, not my type?" Too late, I realized that I had fallen into a trap and chided myself. "This isn't a question about 'type,'

I'm just curious about his work in *taro*. You know the usual stuff; school, politics, plans. Actually, I could care less about his personal life." After all, his girlfriend had given me a good handle on those details.

Sarang, ever reluctant to indulge in gossip, gave me the headlines. Lono Nooner had done well for himself. He graduated with a degree in agriculture management just as local, sustainable products became popular. Now he was the plantation manager. He occasionally spoke at grower conferences as part of his job.

With this information, I decided to visit Māko's again. I loaded Wharf in the Mustang and left Sarang—at her insistence—working in her garden. Sure, I was heading there to garner information, but if there were fresh malasadas, I'd be a fool not to have some.

However, rather than staying to talk story and munch on malasadas, I left Māko's immediately when the first thing Ruth told me was that Goldswaithe had arrived. She said that half the town was at the plantation co-op to hear him, the other half to heckle him. I skipped the city hall stop and instead drove to the botanical garden opposite the *taro* farm's headquarters.

Government vehicles monopolized the parking lot, forcing locals to park alongside the road. Goldswaithe was mid-speech as the crowd milled around, using the televised moment as more of a block party than a serious attempt to address local problems associated with the forest fires.

Firefighters huddled behind the Secretary of the Environment; their formerly filthy yellow shirts freshly laundered with firm creases on the sleeves. Even their pump truck cast reflections off its glittering chrome. I shielded my eyes with one hand while I squinted at the joker on stage. Maybe I wasn't being fair.

"Hey, Aloha. What are you doing here? Not looking for love again are you?" A woman I vaguely remembered from my youth spoke from the shade of a nearby tree. She held an eighty-ounce refillable cup in one hand, a cigarette in the other, and on her back, she wore a sleeping baby in a backpack. Though the woman was white, the baby was Hawaiian, as were her other three children, currently busy climbing in a *plumeria* tree's lower branches.

From the ground up, she was a remarkable sight. Lace-up leather boots transitioned to skintight jeans that would make a tailor blanch. The backpack pulled mightily on the already overworked buttons of her shirt. It was like a dam trying to hold back the flood.

When not making snide comments, she sucked on her cigarette, the lines on her face adding a certain *je ne sais quoi* to a twenty-year-old case of acne. Her long stringy dishwater blonde hair, woven in the fingers of the baby, was her crowning and most resplendent feature.

I wasn't sure how to answer her slur, although I was confident she was referring to Brother Love's death. Her comment unearthed the history I had hoped to avoid.

"Are these your kids?" I asked. Hey, don't all women like to talk about their kids?

"Who else's would they be?" She punctuated this question with a long draw from her smoke, followed by an even longer pull from her drink.

Sheesh! Someone was a little cranky. Then I remembered her. She had threatened to kill me when I had once told her to quit snaking me on waves a long time ago. I had lived in terror for a week and then had forgotten about it until now. She was flipping crazy then. It didn't seem like she'd had treatment since.

I slipped my sunglasses on—the perfect disguise.

"Well, good to see you again." I moved about ten feet closer to the action. Over my shoulder, I heard the words "kiss ass." I couldn't remember the woman's name, but I had some things I'd like to call her too. Good thing I was going to give up swearing.

Again, I eased closer to the speaker and heard Goldswaithe say, "I promise you these fires will be controlled as soon as we build more dams for water retention."

That was all the hecklers needed to begin their taunts.

"Guess you shouldn't have taken us to court," yelled a teen who looked almost old enough to vote. Chances were Goldswaithe might listen to a constituent, but not a kid.

"How's that gonna work?" This came from someone closer to the stage.

"Go back to DC," was shouted from behind me.

I turned to see who yelled that gem and was rewarded with a middle finger salute from the woman drinking under the tree. Big surprise.

The jibes digressed in tone and content, while the laughter and listeners covering their mouths in embarrassment, increased. Still, I gave Goldswaithe credit for persistence. He delivered his speech directly into the waiting eyes and ears of the television news audience. He was a trained politician looking for a nice film clip and sound bite in front of the desperate locals.

Oh, yeah, he felt their pain. He commiserated with their problems. He could hardly wait to get back on the government helicopter and fly to Honolulu for a lovely dinner in one of the city's five-star restaurants. He would designate Hana a disaster area and later return the funds to Congress during budget negotiations as a token of good faith.

As Goldswaithe left the podium, I watched Kāwika Padriac murmur something to him. Then Padriac led Goldswaithe through the side entrance to the farm's office complex. A handful of security people and local leaders followed. Padriac appeared to be one of few locals amidst the government contingency. I recognized two of the Nooner brothers, Kāne, and Lono, along with some other people from the plantation, heading to the parking area.

As I shadowed them, bits of their conversation reached me. I heard what sounded like "Ew-ee-la." My hearing still sent me faulty messages on occasion.

As we reached the parking area, I heard the helicopter's rotors increase their velocity. The pitch rose, as did the aircraft. Goldswaithe was gone.

I hoped that Kāwika had time to see me. Using the main entrance, I was surprised to see him with Lono in the corridor beyond the reception desk. I thought I picked up the words: Arson, accident and controlled-burn.

Chapter Sixteen

"Kāwika!" I walked up to shake his hand. "I was hoping to see you." My words and smile were genuine. Today his eyes shifted from a steely gaze to twinkle-mode in a moment. Interesting. His hair, that once had been a crown of black curls now showed glimmers of gray. It was his only sign of aging and it made him even more attractive. I blushed.

He gave me the once-over as well.

"Aloha Jones! Wow, long time no see!" He quickly turned to the other man to introduce me. "Aloha, do you remember Lono Nooner?"

"Sure I do." Shaking his hand, I looked him in the eye and said, "Didn't I see you diving at the dam this morning?"

He dropped my hand. "That's a restricted area. What were you doing diving at the dam?"

I tried again. "I was working. What about you?"

"I wasn't there," he said. Then he turned to Kāwika. "If you'd like me to get back to you later with a solid answer, I'd be happy to. That way I won't interrupt you and Aloha. I need to gather up the files, so if you'll excuse me…"

Closing the door of the office, he left us standing in the hall.

"So, Aloha, working hard or hardly working?" Kāwika filled the awkward moment with one of his usual inane comments. Seems everyone was still too polite to ask him to knock it off. I guess each of us has one or two glaring flaws.

"Glad to see you're still here. What's going on with you these days?" He hadn't expected an answer, so my rough segue didn't faze him.

"Same old stuff, different day." SOSDD. A classic. He gave himself a good laugh at his wit. With his head back and eyes closed, he didn't see me grimace. He was so darned good looking and smart that I figured he used a little dorkiness to be more approachable.

"Any other homes in danger from the fire?" I asked.

"No. But we had a lot of resource go up in flames." He reluctantly buckled down to a real conversation. "The co-op owns most of the upstream land so we can control the water. Without the plant biomass we'll get too much sediment in the *lo'i*."

"I guess you can't control lightning strikes."

He blanched, then, said, "Nope, just like in fishing, farming and logging, you can't control Mother Nature or machinery." Then he glanced at his watch.

"I guess you need to go, huh?" I had nothing. I don't want to appear conceited but I am reasonably good-looking, smart, and single. Usually this combo brought some interest, but never with Kāwika. "What were you saying to Goldswaithe as he left the stage that made him mad?"

Kāwika's eyes went steely again. "Let's just say I was making sure our resources get reimbursed. Nice to see you Aloha, but I have a call to make. Say 'Hi' to Sarang for me. I sure miss seeing her at cooperative meetings."

He lifted his hand in a slight wave and booked down the hall.

Hmm, I had no idea Sarang had quit going to co-op meetings. The various *taro* farmers had banded together for marketing their products. Her husband Frank's family had been part of the collective. As Frank's sole heir, Sarang held a fractional ownership in his family's *lo'i*. I knew she would tell me nothing. However, Auntie Ruth was a font of information with more answers than questions.

I moseyed through the co-op's administrative area, peering into offices and generally being nosy. Then I perused some informative posters on the *taro* plant's lifecycle.

The next poster showed the historic increase in *taro* production because of the dam system. I looked to me like this type of farming would be extinct if not for the efforts made in controlling the water. It even showed a surplus. Growers were producing more than needed to supply the local market. More supply than demand always drive prices down, meaning less profit for the farmers. Hmm… Something worth considering.

I checked my watch. Time to go.

Back in the car, I told Wharf, "I have no idea what's going on around here anymore." As usual, my faithful companion offered me the right mix of comfort and motivation. He rested his massive head on my shoulder. A quick smooch on his nose ended the magic moment. He crossed the seat, shoved his head out the window, and let his ears flap in the breeze. A trace of saliva trailed down his jaw and whipped away in the wind.

When I braked to a halt in a shaded space in front of city hall, he immediately returned to horizontal happiness.

"Boy, if this isn't the saddest excuse for architecture, I don't know what is." I said to him, a moment before he dozed off.

As usual, I had enough opinions for both of us. I appreciated the economy of the project, but from top to bottom, the concept was a compromise. Even to the most untrained eye, it was obvious that no one would appreciate the result.

I left the windows at half-mast for my already slumbering partner.

At the reception desk sat the geekiest Hawaiian I'd ever seen. Probably in his early twenties, he wore his hair in a crew cut, sported tortoiseshell spectacles, and dressed like preppy was back in style. His nametag said Tom Baptiste. Must be a descendant of Dirty Face Baptiste. I didn't know anyone from that side of the family had come back to the Islands. Interesting.

I introduced myself as Sarang's sister. "I'd like to read the minutes from this year's council meetings." I was sure that he would put me off.

"Public records, you know, have at 'em." He pointed to an adjoining room lined with bookshelves. It included an eclectic mix of resources.

"Let me know if you need to make copies of any of the minutes." The telephone began ringing and he excused himself, shutting the door as he left the room.

I pulled the current volume and skimmed the minutes in reverse chronology. Names from my past popped up throughout. A few I did not recognize had become key speakers on various issues within the town.

Still, I was frustrated. What was the point of this exercise? I wasn't finding anything of value and probably wasting my time.

My sister wasn't a council member, but she regularly attended the meetings and voiced her opinions until about three months earlier. Other than that, the only item of any interest was the approval of a scuba class for one local law enforcement person. I guessed it was Lindy.

In the previous year's records, I recognized a pattern of statements and interruptions from a group that wanted more restrictions for environmental reasons. On the face of it, the minutes indicated that the group had their concerns heard. In reality, if the local council was like any other political body. Most likely, its members thought they had smoothed a few ruffled feathers and hoped the friction would dissolve. I had a hunch they were wrong. Time to go.

In Buffy, Wharf was still collapsed across the black leather back seat. He raised his head when I unlocked the door, then dropped back into a deep slumber. The inside of the car was terribly hot, even though I'd left each window down several inches. Wharf would have been better off at Sarang's in the shade with a cool bucket of water at his side.

I opened the doors and rubbed his belly until he inverted and stretched. What a good boy. He helped my angst, he filled my heart with love, he had no time for judgment, and he loved me despite my many flaws. I guessed Stinger offered the same comfort to Sarang, but apparently, it wasn't enough. We needed to talk.

I was feeling dissatisfied with myself. So far, I'd been no help to Sarang. My dive investigation was progressing slowly, if at all. Certainly, my relationships with people in Hana were far from idyllic.

Ten minutes of rumination didn't help my mood as I drove the dirt roads back to the cabin. The sun had passed over the ridge behind the house. The yard surrounding the cabin was now a peaceful glade. 'ukulele music filtered through the open doors and windows, as light breezes mingled the scents of burnt brush, freshly cut grass and barbecued chicken. Somehow, those smells offered me the serenity I had lacked moments before.

I extricated Wharf from the car, gave him water, kisses, and the comfort he so deserved. Holding him close, I inhaled the scent of his fur and he consoled me with his soft warm nuzzling. I could feel tears coming as I entered the cabin.

Sarang was at the sink, chipping cabbage for Coleslaw. She glanced up as I entered, then gave me the open-armed hug that was absent at my first return. A faded cotton sleeveless shirt matched her old jeans. Now I noticed that her skin color was more wan than tan. The look on her face sang of concern, loneliness, and longing.

"What happened?" Sarang asked, unafraid of directness despite her ban on gossip.

"I don't know. I guess I've been gone so long that I don't belong anymore." Briskly I added, "Of course, it's not that I want to belong, anyway." *Liar, liar, pants-on-fire*, trilled my subconscious teen. She was really starting to piss me off. Then I realized I was trying to stop swearing and she'd goaded me into it. I think she stuck her tongue out.

"You don't need to belong, nor do you need to be away. This community is not a private club, nor is the town. You are who and what you are. No one can take that away from you. Besides, you will always belong in this home."

She kept one arm around my waist as she spoke, looking directly in my eyes, searching my very soul. I looked away, knowing that words could not alleviate my feelings of dread. I attributed this to a time of personal metamorphosis from which I would grow. I kept those words to myself and kissed Sarang on the cheek.

"Are you ready for dinner? I made your favorites, teriyaki chicken, sticky white rice, coleslaw and macaroni salad." She turned the conversation in a safer direction.

"I could smell it as I came in. Thank you so much for asking me to come back. It was the right thing to do, even though I haven't done a darn thing to help."

"Setting the table would help." She didn't allow me even a moment of self-pity. "I thought we'd eat out on the deck tonight."

Stinger and Wharf hunkered down under the picnic table during the meal, silently hoping for fallen tidbits. I was running my bare foot over Wharf's back when I said, "I stopped at the co-op today. The entry display and the library are impressive."

"We got a grant for some of it," Sarang said. "The council even added a line item to the budget for maintaining the library." She dunked a potato chip in ranch dressing. An errant glop hit the deck. Wharf raised his eyebrows. Stinger licked it up without lifting her head. Years had smoothed the surface, allowing her to avoid a painful tongue splinter.

"I skimmed the council minutes for the last couple of years to catch up on the politics." I left a nice long pause, chewing the sweet coleslaw like a bunny, and hoped that Sarang might volunteer details on the hot topics. I underestimated my sister's wisdom. She rewarded me with silence—so much for the subtle approach.

"Seems like there's quite a bit of controversy within the town about the dam." I scooped up the last few chips.

"Are you asking me my opinion?" Sarang asked, as she rested her elbows on the table.

"Well, yeah, I guess I am." I smiled and shielded my eyes from the amber light of the setting sun.

"The dams have created tremendous power—both hydroelectric and political. First, they created jobs, then electricity, then irrigation, then recreation. This all adds up to money.

"Then the other kind power came into play. Some say the dams cost this region's original inhabitants one of their most valued resources. As Islanders, we are ineffably linked to the water. Hawaiians lose more than money when the *taro* becomes extinct. They become extinct as a culture."

"The *taro* isn't extinct, Sarang," I wasn't looking for an argument, but I still wanted to maintain some perspective. "At the farm, I read that the harvest rates are aligning with historical numbers."

"Aloha, what you don't realize is that those rates are based on drastically reduced numbers to begin with. Five million years of *taro* genetics are being flushed down the drain in fifty years of genetic modification."

Without even realizing it, Sarang had adopted the jargon of those who negotiated these issues, no longer on the sidelines. She used the same verbal and body language that had become her trademark as a military interrogator—take no prisoners.

"These are fundamental rights, not special rights. Our town signed on to the *For the Sake of the* Taro *Charter*, even though a few among us wanted a different solution, a permanent solution. For now, I must stand by the council's decision."

A sense of not belonging again enveloped me. I had read the issues from a sterile distance. My personal future did not ride on the town's coattails. I made my own way in life and never looked back. Now I saw that there was more to being local than just skin color.

Sarang said, "Get the bureaucrats, politicians, and special interests away from the table and let unbiased scientists evaluate the species

133

ecology. Plus, we need to keep educating the next generation about the ancient culture."

"Why not remove the dams and let things go back to the way they were?" I had to ask the billion-dollar question. Everywhere in the Islands, you hear someone on one or the other side of this debate. Pure environmentalists strut with signs calling for dam removal. Electric power industry representatives paper the streets with propaganda outlining the benefits of their jobs, and then they lay off the workers and sell the power for a profit. The wealth of windmills left surpluses during the day and shortages in peak hours. It wasn't a perfect marriage.

"That's only part of the solution. You know as well as I do that there used to be some serious waterfalls, channels and natural dams for the water to navigate." Sarang continued her lesson.

"The problem is split so many ways. We need more habitat protection, no more of these 'controlled burns' and no grazing to the streams. We need to get rid of the huge reservoirs behind the dams, get less sediment and cooler temperatures in the river." Sarang took a breather. "Of course, other things would cost less, both in actual dollars expended and in funds lost. It's totally crazy."

My look spoke volumes.

"Yeah, Aloha, even the word 'crazy' is improper these days. I should know."

Chapter Seventeen

The word brought Mallory's death back to my mind and I abruptly switched topics. "I guess the service is tomorrow." Immediately I wished that I'd learned more about the funeral.

"Are you going?" She squinted as she asked the big money question.

"Yeah, I'm picking Lindy up at ten. You want to ride with us?"

Sarang hesitated. I didn't understand. Funerals were *de rigueur* in Hana. It didn't matter what happened during life. At death, all bets were off. "Stay away from the funeral Aloha. Don't go looking for trouble," she said.

"Sarang..." I stopped my snotty don't-tell-me-what-to-do reply. "It's my duty to myself to attend. Maybe it will help me bury the past."

"Then I'll go with you," she said. Sarang picked up her plate and went to the kitchen.

I followed with mine. As we began washing, rinsing and drying the dishes side-by-side, I damned the torpedoes and shifted the conversation into personal mode.

"Sarang, when did the PTSD start?" It was an honest question.

"When Frank was killed in action, it was the last straw. Something broke, some gear in my mind that I used to control my emotions. After that, Aloha, I did things, I saw things while I was doing interrogations, things that I want to forget but I can't."

Each of my sisters and I had joined a different branch of the military with vastly different careers. Our oldest sister, Liebe, after retiring from the Air Force, went on to work for the airlines. For our next sister, Amoré, a public information officer in the Navy, controlling words and imagery was her prime directive. Sarang became a Marine, as did her husband Frank. I retired early from the Coast Guard a year ago after an underwater explosives incident that cost me my hearing in one ear. Our sister Love was still a drummer in the Army's marching band. Our youngest sister, Viva, apparently for lack of the availability of another branch of the military, joined the Peace Corps.

Lost in thought, and my bad ear nearest Sarang, I nearly missed her next statement.

"Roy is the only person who really understands."

Cowboy Roy? He was just a latter-day veteran turned hippie with his own unique perspective on everything.

"What do you mean?" I asked, as I moved dishes from the drainer to the cabinet, drying them along the way.

"He's not weird you know. He's just like me."

I couldn't see it. Apparently, it was the end of the conversation. Sarang called to Stinger and they both shuffled off to bed.

I wondered what had just happened. While I pondered, Wharf wandered off to the doggie latrine, out of the yard, and behind a spindly Norwalk pine for the illusion of privacy. When he returned, we made our way into the cabin's security.

Only after sacking-out did I notice that the smell of fresh mowed grass mingled with the scent of the other kind of grass. Was my sister smoking a medicinal marijuana cigarette? On the other hand, was some neighbor kid toking on a blunt?

No matter the reason—the act was illegal. For me—despite my own stupid mistakes as a teen—it was just plain wrong. I stormed into Sarang's room fueled with good intentions, carried by a bad attitude.

Sarang had her cell phone cradled between her shoulder and ear while she sat with her back to the head board, her bare feet stretched over a Hawaiian quilt with a pattern of dolphins. With a word, she hung up. I stood silent, hands at my sides, my emotional balloon deflated.

"Yes?" She gave me the chance to avoid embarrassment.

"I smelled smoke." Lame, but true.

Sarang's feet hit the floor in motion. She bolted past me. I followed. She stood in the middle of the clearing, her head tilted back, eyes closed, nose assessing the air. "No smoke." She reverted to her preferred verbal shorthand.

"Uh," I needed to think fast. Did I want to accuse her of smoking pot or did I want to let it go?

She walked a path that seemed well worn, as though she had a security ritual. A mental checklist. Was it part of how she handled the PTSD? She surprised me with her next question. "Feeling guilty?"

I'm not famous for my poker face, but I gave it a shot. Yeah, I have some guilt, about a variety of things. "No." I denied. "Why should I feel guilty?" I thought she was talking about the smelling smoke question. Little did I know.

Sarang simply shook her head as she walked through the fine dust of her path and up the porch stairs. Inside, she immediately crossed into her bedroom and closed the door, a not-so-subtle signal that our conversation had ended.

I watched the sky darken out the window and pondered her situation. The song *Nothin' From Nothin' Leaves Nothin'* looped through my brain. I consider it a flaw to have such a weak mind that anyone can get me with a song. Snake used to do it on purpose. Usually with just a slice of the chorus, I'm hooked.

I patted Wharf's head in appreciation that he couldn't get songs into my head. Then he and I curled up on the couch, his face resting on my feet. I could feel my pulse against his massive jawbone. His eyes, the color of chocolate milk, watched me. I went to sleep feeling his breath on my ankle. His presence, protection from my dreams.

In Hana, funerals, weddings, and graduations are replayed in detail at Māko's and Pau Hana—the best parts reviewed as seriously as an instant replay on televised football.

It was the first time in years I had entered a church. A choir sang of Jesus eating the bread of His disciples. The six Tongan women's voices, accompanied by a guitarist, blended perfectly; as though they'd been singing together for a millennium.

Each pew held a handful of mourners—or at least spectators. Small town funerals function as social occasions as much as memorials. To me, the remarkable magenta shag carpet and the altar draped in matching fabric with gold trim seemed more gaudy than Godly.

Sarang, Lindy, and I were ushered to a center pew. The location signified that we were not family, but deference given to Sarang's position in the community.

"Nate looks better than he has in years." Lindy pointed toward the front row. "It's like he had a load lifted off his chest."

Hmm. "Who's that with him?" I whispered, referring to a striking woman with stylish glasses and a good haircut and color, singing along beside him. She reminded me of a bird-of-paradise: Crisp, colorful, finely formed and full-throated.

"That's Mallory's mom."

She looked different from when she'd photographed me years before. It hadn't been a moment when I focused on her. Instead, and rightly so, I had been intent on reviving Brother Love.

Eyeing the woman, Sarang furrowed her brow. Her thoughts echoed mine: Like mother, like daughter.

Now we all sang *Amazing Grace*—how ironic. I always thought I could see everything, read faces, maybe minds, and turns out—now, I'm blind—at least to Mallory's killer. Trying to be inconspicuous, I glanced around to see whom else I might recognize. Everyone I had already seen since coming home was there, including the two jerks from the paper and Haspin. They all wore their summer Sunday best, except Haspin, who wore his work uniform—complete with a Sam Brown holster. His black leather, basket-weave belt packed a Glock, an Asp, a VHF radio, pepper-spray, two handcuffs and two ammo clips with 250-grain, hollow-point, and yellow jacket "muck-em-up-bad" bullets. This particular piece of art hung slightly below the prescribed waistline, resulting in a hint of plumber's butt. If Haspin ever fell in the water, he'd sink like a brick—not, I'm almost, but not quite, ashamed to say, an unpleasant thought.

The lights dimmed as a minister and two girls walked down the center aisle; the girls carrying candle-lighters.

The Nooner clan sat together on the opposite side of the church near the back row. Lindy seemed to have a particular interest in their activities.

As the reverend spoke, quiet weeping arose from those in the pews. With increasing frequency, I heard "amen" murmured around us. Nearly everyone jumped out of his or her skin when Mallory's mother jumped up and screamed. "Oh Jesus! Oh God! Why did you take my babies?" Her arms and fingers strained to the heavens. Several other women sprang to their feet, echoing her words. "Oh Jesus! Oh Jesus! Oh Jesus!" They, too, swayed with emotion. The cool sanctuary heated rapidly as the Pentecostal aerobics session took its toll on the AC.

My entourage sank lower into our seats, finding it increasingly difficult to remain inconspicuous while not participating in the human conflagration around us.

Raised with a combination of my father's Lutheran upbringing and my mom's reliance on a single Mother Earth, I was less than comfortable with the service. None of us had experienced anything like it.

"Sister Mallory walks with Jesus," sang the pastor.

"Amen!" The congregation was getting into it now.

"Oh, Lord, lead her home!" Louder with each verse, his voice echoed through the sanctuary. The crowd took over with abandon.

"Hallelujah!"

"Amen!"

"Praise the Lord!"

"Amen!"

"Take her home, Lord!"

"Amen!"

"You killed her!"

Silence…

The reverend, intent on swaying, sweating and singing out, took a moment too long to gather himself together. The noise had grown so loud that the accuser was invisible. Still, everyone warily turned around, peering over each other's shoulders, trying to identify the voice.

Silence…

Visibly shaken, the reverend chose to punt. "Her death brings forth goodness. As in all you do, Lord, something wonderful has come of this tragedy. As Mallory reunites with Missy, an anonymous angel has donated one-thousand-dollars cash, in Missy's name, for cancer research."

So much for my quiet donation. I wondered if the Nagasakos had told him why I had the money to give.

As though electrified, the minister's arms, shoulders and head jutted upright from his solemn downcast position. Theatrical effects were no stranger to this man. He ended with both hands in the air, eyes closed and back arched. Then he said, "Go! Leave your lives of sin. And sin no more."

The "Amens," "Praise Jesus'" and "Hallelujahs" erupted throughout the room. The organist launched into the recessional—those in back ushered out first.

This gave me plenty of time to watch Nate and Mallory's mother cling together. The pastor rested a hand on the shoulder of each. I suspected he had all the warmth of a wet fish. He masked this with plenty of body contact. I imagined that the pastor liked being the fence his female congregation leaned on. Sadly, I realized that I was doing what I most deplored about organized religion—I was judging others. It was like being racist, just making decisions based on a certain look.

Perhaps he had spoken directly to me. My personal growth continued with each passing revelation. How could I have remained so rigid in my own thinking? These thoughts plagued, yet pleased me. It felt good to grow. Some truths stayed in my former scales of black and white, while some veered daringly close to gray.

These musings caused me to shiver as I fell into line with the other mourners. Already, they filled vehicles with illuminated headlights and motors running, while Mallory was loaded into the waiting hearse. Pomp exuded from each bereaved breath. This was Hana at its best.

While we waited in the car for the procession to begin, I was surprised to see Dr. Pease, my sister's psychiatrist, in what appeared to be a search for his vehicle. He wove through row after row and from car to car. "Hey, Sarang, there's Dr. Pease. What he's doing here?"

"He used to work with Mallory," Lindy inserted, from the back seat. She was picking long, yellow dog hair from her skirt.

"Where was that?" I wondered aloud.

"Mallory worked at the clinic—she transcribed records, which means she knew everything about everybody—she was there, day and night."

Lindy's episode of flicking and flinching continued. The dog hairs were like a magnet to the gray fabric of her dress. Her expression evolved from disdain to anger.

I watched her in the mirror. Caught, Lindy dropped her hands and shrugged. At that instant, the heat generated by the idling vehicle caused me to crank up the fan. A plume of fur fluttered through the car. Still, my thoughts were elsewhere.

Why did someone else think Mallory had been murdered? Twice now, I'd heard the statement, "You killed her." Was Mallory's death an accident? If not, then why was she a victim? Victims are rarely chosen at random, by an unknown assailant, despite Hollywood's efforts to scare the public into believing otherwise.

The husband or lover—present or former—is the usual culprit. Although Mallory and Nate were divorcing, my experience with Nate told me that he was not a violent man. It appeared that Mallory's mother gave her adequate support. Even Mallory's mysterious relationship with Kāne Nooner lacked overtones of abuse, jealousy or anger. Although drowning is the fourth highest cause of accidental death each year, murdering someone by drowning is not an easy task.

The more I thought about it, the more nagging questions bumped my brain. I still didn't know why Mallory was diving at the dam. I hadn't yet seen the photographs from her camera. Where had Mallory gotten the scuba equipment? I hated to do it, but I needed to ask Lindy about the police department investigation.

"Lindy?" I said. "Without your violating the integrity of the investigation, can you tell me what the department's come up with on Mallory's death?"

"What investigation?" She asked. "As far as I know, Gommer declared her death an accidental drowning. Haspin hasn't asked anyone about why she was diving alone. Seems like it's an open and slut case."

I almost missed her slip-of-tongue. I glanced in the mirror to see her smirk. Instead, while she still worked on the dog hair, if anything, she looked relieved. Must be the "I hate paperwork and court" syndrome.

We found a place to park on the cemetery's lush lawn. A canvas canopy marked the location of the burial where a few people sat in folding chairs. The other mourners stood behind the chairs, facing Haleakalā's smoke-shrouded shoulders.

Lost in my thoughts, the majority of the burial proceeded in what seemed like seconds. Only when I heard murmured "Amens" did I remember where I was, as Mallory's mother tossed flowers into the gaping hole.

My eyes focused on Haspin chatting with Dr. Pease. Beyond them, the Nooner clan remained together—yet separate from the other mourners. The Nagasakos—wizened and weary—walked toward the circular drive, a young woman in a smart suit between them. The two newsroom trolls slouched along behind. It continued to infuriate me that their daughter Dee Dee had sold the photo of Brother and me to the tabloids.

I wanted to ask Lindy where Dee Dee ended up, but when I looked around for her, she was with the Nooners. With my observation antennae so raised, I was surprised when I heard Nate's voice at my shoulder.

"Nice view, huh?" he said, about an inch from my ear, referring to the ocean in the distance, while softly grasping my elbow.

"Nate!" Instinctively, I pulled away, and while trying not to appear shaken, I said, "How are you doing?"

He laughed at startling me. I wanted to kick him in the knees, or worse. Of course, I'd had that desire for years.

"Okay, I guess."

He stopped laughing. "I do fine for awhile, then, everything falls to pieces." He glanced to the marble tableau marking his daughter's grave. "I used to think I had it all, and I did. Now I have nothing."

"Nate, this hurt will last forever, but your life will get better. I promise you." I empathized with his pain, but didn't feel I was the best person to comfort him.

"I used to think that my heart would break every second when we lost Missy. I'll never forget her." He closed his eyes. "Most of my memories of her are happy now, not sad."

"At least Mallory didn't have to endure the suffering of cancer."

"Neither did Missy." He looked off toward the mountains, while he wiped tears from his face.

"What?" Okay, I was about to pop this guy right in the nose if he lied to me one more time.

He apparently didn't see my expression as he continued to vent. "Well, the chemotherapy was awful, but she was really doing pretty well and we thought she would recover. Then one day, she just dropped off. It can happen with leukemia—the body's resistance is down and a slight infection can overpower the whole system."

His last statement sounded like one he'd heard and simply repeated. I tried again. "Still, it's good that neither of them suffered."

"I don't know about Mallory, but when I found Missy, she was lying there in my bed, so peaceful…" he swallowed a sob.

Against my better judgment, I hugged him and herded him toward the hearse. As we reached the car, an unfamiliar voice assaulted me.

"Well, you didn't wait long to pick up where you left off, did you?"

I turned to see Mallory's mother. Ignoring her, I spoke softly to Nate. "Take care. It will get better. Let me know if there's anything you need."

Without looking at my attacker, I sought out Lindy and Sarang, urging them to leave.

"Don't ever leave me alone with him again." My jaw clenched and hands splayed at my sides, I gave them the go-to-the-car-look with my eyes.

Lindy and Sarang had no idea what I was talking about and their confused expressions forced me to explain. "With Nate. Don't ditch me like that again. Mallory's mom even got her claws into me."

Sarang knew too well the consequences of interactions with that woman. She blamed her for my self-imposed sabbatical from Hana. A look of resolve set on her face as we trudged to my car.

Chapter Eighteen

At the car, I was delighted to see that I had a message from Eddie on my cell phone. I dialed his number as I drove. I would play it cool since I had Sarang and Lindy in the car.

"I'm returning your call."

"Wait a second," he said, probably the nature of his day, but not a great greeting. I'd left a message asking him to check with his friend in the Honolulu crime lab for the results of the air analysis in Mallory's scuba tank.

"He said the smell of garlic was his first clue." Eddie—ever the food hound—said. "Whatever it is, you better bring me some."

"Garlic, huh?" I muttered. "Anything else?" I wanted to know if I'd missed anything interesting in Lahaina.

"I heard a drunk fell off his boat," he paused.

I shuttered, thinking of the body I'd found there my first week back in the Islands.

Then he said, "By the time marine patrol got there, he was puking and kissing the ground."

"Fly down?" I asked the usual question. Most of our drunk drowning victims die taking a whiz. Their little boats capsize, and with their mind and motor control impaired, they try to save their ice chest first. Big mistake.

"Yep." Eddie ran through some other gossip while I listened. I gradually depressed the accelerator, my reflexes speeding ahead with my thoughts. Not until I saw the lights flashing in my rear-view mirror and looked at my speedometer did I realize I was speeding.

"Uh-oh," I said, as I pulled over, "Gotta go."

Eddie didn't ask why. I wanted to ask him if he'd heard anything about the investigation into my forced leave of absence, but didn't have time.

When I saw Haspin emerge from the patrol car, my pulse raced.

Apparently, not concerned about any previous warrants on my vehicle, he didn't stay in his rig long enough to run the plates. As I watched him in my side mirror, I saw him hike up his wayward slacks. No matter what the situation, I didn't want to see those pants drop. An involuntary shudder shivered up my spine.

"Well, look who we have here," Haspin said, when he approached my open window.

I put on my best sheepish look, and attempted to pander to his ego. "Boy am I glad you stopped me. I was just asking Lindy where we might find you." The darkened windows blotted Lindy and Sarang from his view until he looked through the driver's side to see them.

"Officer Somers, it sure wouldn't look good on your record to be the passenger in a vehicular homicide."

Lindy responded with a puzzled look while I filled in the blanks.

"Are you saying that we killed someone? Cripes, I'm kind of embarrassed that I missed it." Surely, sarcasm wouldn't remedy the situation, but neither had blatant sucking up.

"Let me see your license." As an afterthought, Haspin mumbled, "please." I gave him my wallet, with the license visible.

"Take it out." As he handed it back to me, an old photo of me posing with Nate at a Halloween party slipped from my wallet. Taken well before Nate dumped me, I kept it because I loved the mermaid costume I had made for the occasion.

"So what do we have here?" Haspin could hardly contain his glee. "Looks to me like you have a little conflict-of-interest in this case, Miss Jones.

Maybe you should step back to my vehicle where we can chat privately."

Reluctantly, I followed him, signaling Lindy to come along. There was no way I wanted a few minutes alone with Haspin.

At his car, I leaned my backside on the bumper. Although I tried to put on a confident front, I had both my arms and legs crossed, telegraphing my nervousness through body language.

"This has nothing to do with you, Sommers."

He pulled out his tiny notebook and then checked his watch to note the time. Without looking at either of us, he asked, "Do you think it was appropriate for you to perform the body recovery on the Deems woman, considering your relationship with her husband?"

Though my stomach was brewing a vat of anxiety, I spoke in a calm, clear voice. "I am a member of the state's Water Rescue Team. Our mission statement includes assisting all jurisdictions in rescue, recovery, and investigation. You called me. I have no relationship with the deceased's husband. If you have questions about my qualifications, too bad. If you have a problem with the manner, in which I handled my duties, too bad. If I have broken any laws, you need to read me my rights. But, if you want to hassle someone, you're picking on the wrong person." Then to punctuate my sentence I added, "Dog."

He gave up on taking notes. Lindy didn't say a word. I wondered what his next move would be.

He took the smart way out. "Hey, no harm, no foul. I thought I should check. Oh, and you better get that speedometer checked or lighten up on the gas. I really wouldn't want to see a former public servant get a citation." Hitching up his pants, he climbed into his own vehicle and drove away.

Uh oh, it seemed like the news of my racial profiling investigation had reached Hana.

Lindy and I did not discuss the encounter with Haspin. Some things are not fixable. At the station, she moved her stuff to her patrol car. Sarang and I headed home to our fur fan club.

On the way, we talked stress. We always covered the same ground. I would ask, "How are you feeling today? Did you take your medicine? Is it making you sick? Is there anything I can get you?"

Sarang's answers were typically, "Fine. No. No. No."

I finally worked up the courage to ask the toughest question. "Are you growing your own weed, or buying it?"

"That's none of your business," she snapped.

"Where are you getting it?"

"I won't discuss this with you." She pursed her lips and glared out the side window.

"Sarang, it doesn't matter whether you produce it or use it. In this country, it's still illegal."

"I've given everything I have to this country. You don't need to tell me what freedoms it's taken from me. I need it to feel better, and there's no reason why I shouldn't use it." She paused, and then added, "Other than the damn government trying to control my every move."

"Yeah, that'll stand up in court." I mocked her.

She gave me that squinty-eye look that says, "Be careful." It was the same look that Stinger gives Wharf right before she nails him to the ground.

"This may sound funny, but I'm not sure I like your relationship with the Nooners. I see you're even siding with them on the local council now. That whole family is trouble. When caught, they'll leave you faster than you can spit. Can't we talk to Dr. Pease about other solutions?"

"Isn't it about time you went back to work?" Sarang's patience had waned.

"Yeah, I think it is. I'll call in tonight." The reality of trying to be Sarang's support system was ruining my prodigal fantasy. Silence prevailed for the remainder of our journey. I neglected to tell her I'd probably lost my part-time job.

Although not friends, Stinger and Wharf barked a nonetheless harmonious duet of greetings from the shaded tin porch.

"Come on, let's go in and talk about this," I said. I'd heard that talking helps. Even if we couldn't reach an agreement, I hoped that we could reach a better understanding of each other's position.

Wharf bounded to my side, his eyes all squinty and his tail wagging his body from side to side. "Hi, Wharfie. What's been going on around here?" He immediately buried his face in my thigh while I scratched his back.

During his ritual reunion with me, Stinger and Sarang shared their own traditional greeting. Stinger was a blur of black fur swishing wildly about Sarang's legs, hopping and nipping for extra morsels of attention.

Afterward, the two old girls—as I liked to think of them—walked to the end of the driveway to collect the mail while Wharf and I waited on the porch, his jowls resting on my lap as I rubbed his ears. I was surprised when Sarang handed me an envelope, especially since it was addressed to Aloha Jones in care of Sarang Jones. The handwriting was familiar. My hands shook and my face flushed as I opened the letter. As I read the words written on the plain white paper, I knew my jitters were warranted. The black scrawl read, *"We know you killed Brother. You'll die for your sins."*

The unsigned note came from straight out of the past. It was very similar to other hate mail I had received shortly after Brother Love's death.

"Sarang, this is just like the letters we got before." I handed it to my sister to read.

Sarang walked with the note without looking back at me. The dogs and I followed her to her desk.

"I kept these in case I ever saw the same handwriting again."

Sarang pulled a file from her desk. I recognized the notes I had received years earlier. Since I had left Hana before the full impact of Brother's death and the photographs, Sarang had kept copies and sent me the originals.

"These are nearly exact," I said. The similarities extended well beyond handwriting—content, language, paper, size—everything was familiar.

"Why does everyone want me to leave again?" A twinge of self-pity edged my voice.

"Not *everyone* wanted you to leave last time. You wallowed in victimization, and I partially blame myself for allowing it. I won't make that mistake again. Life is too short."

"I'm not feeling sorry for myself. You don't know what it's like. It's time for me to go home."

My harangue demanded a grand exit. I didn't exactly slam the door as I left, but I closed it with force. By the bottom step, I realized that I was acting like a spoiled brat. Still, I had too much pride to backtrack. Instead, I went to my car with Wharf on my heels. There I sat, stewing over my own childishness, my anger at being the target of a bully, and at the circumstances of my return to Hana running wild in my psyche.

Nothing was going as I had planned or hoped. It was not simply Sarang's illness: It was about Haspin, the Nagasakos whose handwriting I recognized from the check signature, Mallory, and especially Nate. To blow off steam, I decided to drive down to Māko's. Maybe a dose of grease would cure my attitude.

"… still smoldering on the back side of the ridge." Māko was sharing the latest fire updates with his regulars as he worked his way down the counter refilling coffee mugs. He saluted me as I entered. It was easy to forget about the forest fires that brought me back to Hana until I heard Māko say that some areas were still burning in the next valley.

I mouthed, "Where is Ruth?" Māko waved me toward the office. I poked my head into the closet-sized space where boxes of supplies, bills and catalogues surrounded my aunt.

"Aloha! I was hoping you'd come visit," Ruth said as she hung up the telephone.

Little guilt bugs bit at my brain—I had never been one for visiting, for small talk or for society's subtle niceties. I truly enjoyed Ruth, but my glazed eyes and insincere smile gave me away.

"It's okay. I figured you'd want to hide out, since Sarang already called. She said you pitched a fit and left."

Ruth unstuck her sweaty, wide legs from the vinyl chair, and sought solace with Māko in the kitchen. I closed the door and tried to crank up the air conditioner as I settled in at the desk.

It was time to call in about my accusation of racial profiling. In this case, my boss, Babs McKee, answered on the first ring.

"This is Aloha. Do I still have a job?" It was easy to mouth off to Haspin in Hana, but since the secret was out, I might as well face the charges.

Babs ignored my question. "I got a phone call from the Hana police chief's office." I knew at that moment that she owned me. And, that she planned to make me sweat. "What the heck did you do over there?" She liked this strategy, since it left me a broad picture to paint.

"I didn't do anything. I mean, I did something, but nothing wrong. I mean, I might have done something wrong. I don't think so, but I didn't do it on purpose." Then I paused. "Wait a minute. What do you mean? Why would you think I did anything wrong?" Too late, I realized her trap. Quickly, I said, "Can I call you back? I have another call waiting."

"No you don't. Besides, I am glad you checked in. I did get a call from someone checking your credentials, but after you dove. What's going on over there?"

"Uh, do I still have a job? Can Wharf and I come back to work?"

"Listen, what you said was stupid and probably misinterpreted, but it's out of my hands now. It's my boss's decision." Babs seemed to have the facts worked out, if not the solution.

"What did Dhong ask you?" I was worried about another negative entry in my personnel file.

"It wasn't Dhong. We talked before you did the dive for his department. Some guy named Haspin called to dog you in.

I mentally kicked Haspin in the nuts. What was his problem anyway?

"He had a complaint about Wharf." Babs paused. "He said Wharf threatened him. I knew that was ridiculous Aloha. By the time I finished with him, that pompous little bureaucrat knew you two were the best the department has to offer."

"Really? Geez, Babs, thanks so much. Wharf didn't do anything wrong. Maybe I should drive back tonight." It made a great excuse to leave Hana.

"I don't think so, Aloha. Just give it some time," she said. "How is your sister's home? Did you help her move out before the fires hit? Did the dive mission cause problems? I could have sent someone else over."

"Her place is fine."

I was ready to sleep in my own bed and regain my independence.

Finally, she said, "Since tomorrow is Friday, just stay for the weekend. We'll see you Monday morning."

After the call ended, I debated whether to head home anyway. I wanted to be with Sarang but hated the idea of apologizing. I just wanted the pain to stop. Before I could decide, I heard Ruth's voice and then a timid knock. After pushing the door open a crack, she peered in and said, "Aloha, you have a visitor."

Who would seek me out at Māko's?

Chapter Nineteen

Nate was standing behind Ruth.

"Nate, what do you want?" My tone included my anger at Sarang, along with the rest of the world.

"When I saw your car I decided to stop. Could we talk for a few minutes?" He guided me out of the restaurant and into the back yard.

I still wore the wrinkled cotton dress I had worn to the funeral. My hair, some said my best feature, was back in a ponytail, but my bangs were victims of sweat and frustration. Nate looked better; more relaxed, and had some of his old polish. I was frustrated with my sister, and even my boss for giving me more time off. I wasn't in the mood to soothe Nate.

My pent-up emotions welled to the surface. Nate was in for more of a talk than he expected. I was glad we were outside so our discussion wouldn't add to the local gossip mill.

"What's up?" I focused on Nate as we walked toward the water.

"I wanted to apologize for what my mother-in-law said to you. Whenever Mallory and I had a problem, she always blamed you. She said that I wouldn't have said, done, or acted the same if I'd been with you. No matter how hard I tried, she never trusted me."

Lindy was correct in her assessment. He was looking good, quite different than he had hours earlier. He seemed relaxed, healthy and even hopeful. I saw the person I had once cared for. I wasn't comfortable with the sight.

"I didn't trust you because I saw how quickly you dumped me when the going got tough. I saw how easily you could be manipulated. Get real,

Nate. You're not the injured party here."

As soon as I'd said it, I knew it was not entirely true. Nate and Mallory had lost a child, their marriage, and now, he had lost his wife.

"Aloha, I'm sorry for what I did to you. I know I made a mistake and I'm not even sure that I ever loved Mallory. I want to start over. I want to move forward with my life. I want to have more children."

I stopped breathing for a moment. He had entirely too many needs for my comfort zone.

"Nate, I don't think you understand. I don't want those things, at least not yet—and for sure not with you. I would never trust you. Ever. This is the first time I've ever felt anything in common with Mallory. You can't change affection like underwear."

He didn't even cringe. Instead, he just continued with his list of needs. "I wasn't hitting on you. I have another woman in my life. But, I need your help—I don't think Mallory's death was an accident."

To me, it seemed like he was out of his mind. First, he was a grieving wreck, then despondent and needy, and now, already with a new woman?

"Are you out of your mind? Nate, she was pregnant."

"Mallory had Kāne. Maybe *he* got her pregnant this time. We were getting a divorce. I need to be loved, too."

Again, the injured party? I could hardly keep up with his pathos.

He walked toward the river with his hands in his pockets, jingling keys and change with each step.

"Why does Kāne think you killed Mallory?" I asked as I tossed pebbles into the clear ruffled water.

"It's not my fault." Before I could respond, he added, "Aloha, you're an investigator. What did you find out?"

"They brought me in as a dive specialist. Talk to somebody at the police department." I, too, had questions about the death. "What was she doing diving at the dam, Nate?"

"Ask Kāne, she didn't get into diving until about six months ago. I sort of thought Mal was doing it to compete with you."

"What do you mean... she didn't even know me?"

"Like I said, she had self-esteem problems. She thought I still wanted you, so she tried to be like you. But, it was tough, since she knew how active you are, and she was always sick."

I shuddered... I'd never tried to be someone else. It disturbed me to be the target of such misguided feelings. Did anyone else know of Mallory's problems? To me it seemed her mother knew about, and possibly even shared, Mallory's envy.

"Who knew that she wanted to be like me?"

Nate stopped and gazed across the river to the beach park. Kids were laughing and playing in the shallow water. A couple of dogs paddled after twigs floating along in the current.

"Kāne probably. She didn't have any close girlfriends, but as an only child, she and her mother were close."

None of this seemed to trouble Nate, though I could feel my nerves rippling under my skin. I was outdoors—with vistas on all sides—yet I felt trapped, claustrophobic, and confined.

"I have to get back to Sarang's. If I can, I'll look into the files on Mallory's death. The coroner has already said it was an accident. If I find out anything, I'll let you know."

I tried to think of the right move. Nothing seemed appropriate—from a handshake to a hug, so I simply said, "Good luck, Nate."

I left him standing at the water's edge while I hurried back to my car. If I had been in better shape—physically and emotionally—I would have sprinted, despite the long wrinkled dress.

Inching onto the driver's seat, I turned to Wharf.

"I need a break from Hana and its mental misfits."

The dog nodded sagely as if to say, "How does this make you feel?"

"Even though I'm ticked at Sarang, at least I know she's sane, although struggling to manage and totally misguided about this pot thing." In reviewing the city council meetings, I saw that Sarang often sided with the aging environmentalists who sought militant solutions. I suspected they supplied her with marijuana or, as the locals called it, *pakalōlō*.

"It's time for us to pay them a visit. If they think they can pull a fast one on her, they're wrong." Addicts are addicts. It doesn't matter who they are. They're slaves to their drug.

Then I considered the tainted interactions with the Nagasako family. Hard to believe that they continued to look down at me because of the nude modeling. The old coot at the photo store had shown his distain in a more subtle manner, but his wife, at the paper, was more direct—if pilfering a photo was a sign of disrespect. The conflict at the photo store was easy enough to ignore, but they were crooks at the paper. There wasn't much more I could do. Unfortunately, it caused problems for me at the police department, since the photographs of Mallory were taken on my watch. The last thing I wanted was to be a part of an ongoing investigation in Hana. Or did I?

Like it or not, I was subtly being drawn into Mallory Deems' world prior to her death. I realized that I was driving toward the Nooners' place in hopes of finding out why Mallory was at the dam. It was hardly a coincidence that they were involved with both Mallory and Sarang. Kanaloa had always been a scrapper. I remembered that as a teen he'd had a penchant for trouble—far more than his brothers had. It was likely that he was a frequent "person of interest" in local law enforcement investigations.

Again, using Wharf as my sounding board, I spoke aloud. "I'm not so sure about this police force." Wharf merely blinked.

Each time I'd been around Haspin, I had a strong urge to wash my hands. He reeked of psychological slime—a bully and a bigot toward whites—he seemed incompetent at the least, and criminal at the worst.

Why did Dhong keep him around?

Then there was the mystery diver... what had he been doing?

So, on my list of sane but strained, I had Sarang and Lindy. On my loony list, I had Nate, Haspin and, most certainly, the deceased Mallory. Well, her craziness was over, but it seemed to live on in her mother and maybe in the Nooners, as well.

In my mental review, I kept pushing one person off to the side. Unsure of my feelings toward him, I kept reviewing the moment of Kāwika Padriac's welcome. His warm embrace had felt better than it should, but I hated the very concept of recreating a teenage crush. I wanted to keep that secret. I knew little more about him today than I had years ago, but that mysterious spark was still on fire.

I put my mental misfit list of murder suspects temporarily aside and moved on to another puzzling personality. Why did Dr. Pease allow Sarang to self-medicate with dope? As they said in *The King and I* "It is a puzzlement." In an instant, I decided this question was more pressing than quizzing the Nooners, so I wheeled my car back toward Hana. I wanted to stop this whole thing with Sarang and drugs immediately. Besides, I had far too little information on my sister's treatment and prognosis.

I pushed the speed limit as I drove the back roads into town, hoping Haspin was busy elsewhere. Only as I pulled into town, did I realize that it was nearly five o'clock and that I might be too late to see Dr. Pease.

I had one potential solution in my sights for Sarang's issues. Like a hunting dog on the scent, I chased after it with single-minded focus. In the process, I missed a few prominent signposts pointing to the answers to Mallory's death.

I walked into the psychiatrist's office, where a nurse was sorting through files at the reception desk.

"Is Dr. Pease still in? I'd like to ask him a quick question." I smiled, then widened my eyes and added, "Wow, you sure have your hands full." I hoped mutual commiseration would result in cooperation, even this late in the day. The harried nurse looked down at the multi-button telephone on the desk and said, "He's on the phone right now. Have a seat and I'll let him know that you're here." Then looking back at me, she said, "May I have your name please?"

After I offered her my name, I settled onto a padded chair. It made me think of padded walls. On the table with the obligatory dog-eared magazines, I noticed a loose-leaf notebook. In it were copies of "Getting to Know Us" advertisements placed by the clinic in the local newspaper.

As a means of making the hospital environment more-user-friendly, each page profiled an employee. Near the back of the book, I discovered a page devoted to Mallory. The bio didn't really saying anything about her personal life—no mention of her being a wife or mother. It noted her dedication to the medical community, especially in seeking greater understanding for maladies affecting children. The photo of Mallory was much kinder than those I'd shot. Still, she looked like the Nurse Ratchet of Hana Medical Center—not easy considering her youth. Nevertheless, it did seem that Mallory was truly dedicated to the medical profession.

Since the wait was far longer than I had anticipated, every once in a while, I made eye contact with the nurse again to let her know that I was still waiting. Her beleaguered response was usually a grim smile and a shrug.

Several pages later, I found Dr. Pease's profile. According to the short bio, he was born on Maui, although he'd grown up on Oahu. His father had been one of the original docs in the old clinic.

When I finished the entire book, I flicked back to the page on Mallory. Lost in thought, I jumped when I heard Dr. Pease say my name. He glanced from my face to the page and said, "We'll miss Mallory here at the clinic."

It smelled as though he might have had a cocktail at lunch. Then he popped a mint.

"I came in to talk about my sister's treatment and prognosis." I was trying not to show my anger, frustration and fear. I didn't want to make him defensive. In situations like this, it's best to allow people to come up with the solution I want, and then agree with them.

I followed him into his office where he took control of the conversation. "What are your specific questions?" He gave me his full attention, clasping his hands in front of him on the desk.

"What are the side effects of her illness?"

"I cannot speak to you of Sarang's case specifically but I can tell you classic symptoms among which might apply to her." He sighed, and recited a list from fatigue to suicidal tendencies. His review was textbook perfect. He had dotted his *I*s and crossed his *T*s. He was either covering his bases or well-experienced in generalization and maybe even deceit. It was a determination I hoped to discover.

"What can I do to help?" I asked. I did have the smarts to know that her medications, like all others, are simply a chemistry experiment. Even the doctors wait anxiously to see if they work.

What I heard was, "Blah, blah, blah."

"What about the dope?" I was tired of fishing for answers.

Chapter Twenty

"I don't know what you mean." Pease shrugged.

Suddenly, staying calm was impossible. My pulse quickened. It was like giving a presentation to a roomful of my peers. My knees shook and my face reddened.

"Dr. Pease," my words tumbled out, "You left the room the other day so that you wouldn't have to witness my discussion with Sarang about her marijuana use. I want the truth."

Still, he looked at me with a blank countenance.

"I left the room for your privacy. I know that Sarang uses plant material in her treatment. Of course, I don't subscribe to that, but if it makes her feel better, I support her."

"Listen Doc, it's not about purple coneflower and ginseng. This is about your tacit approval of drug use. It might be legal in Hawai'i, but it's still illegal with the feds. Sarang could go to jail or lose her retirement benefits. How are you going to treat her then?"

The small man rose from behind the desk, his face flushed with tiny sweat beads along his brow. Tightly wound, he resembled a top, ready to propel across the floor in blurred fury. He stood and closed the door, then turned to me.

"Miss Jones," his voice had risen above his examining room whisper, "I am sure you are distraught about your sister's illness. After all, anger is the second step in the grieving process. Although I'm confident, her treatment will proceed well, it is normal to grieve at the illness. But, I do not advocate the use of marijuana in the treatment of my patients. We have plenty of modern medicines to fight the ill effects of PTSD. I've only seen this occur once previously, and for an entirely different reason." As he spoke, I saw his anger diminish and his defenses relax.

On a hunch, I asked, "Why did Missy need dope?"

He clenched his teeth, and I could see his jaw muscles flexing. For a moment, he stood quietly and then said, "You have pushed the boundaries of doctor-client confidentiality too far. If you want your sister checked into the hospital for drug rehabilitation, I'd be happy to assist you. Otherwise, unless you have any other questions about her treatment, I have a prior appointment."

He opened the door and waved me through like a traffic cop.

I had not confirmed that Mallory had used pot on Missy, but I sensed I was on the right track. The "NORMAL" bumper sticker on Mallory's car was a good clue. Now I had a much better idea of the meaning: National Organization for the Reform of Marijuana Laws. The next question had to be; should I ignore the man behind the curtain? The answer was easy—not just no—but "Hell, no!" With that last bit said aloud, I left Dr. Pease no doubt wondering about my intentions.

The cool air and the sun setting low over the horizon reminded me of the time of day. I needed "the cure." I went in search of chocolate milk. Chocolate milk is the fourth of my Life's Great Truths: Chocolate milk cures most ills. The ancillary is that something chocolate with a milk chaser is a poor, yet acceptable substitute.

At Cowboy Roy's Quick Mart I found Lindy and another officer sitting on stools at a counter facing the window—no chocolate in sight. In front of them sat a package of powdered donuts, Lindy's male counterpart nursed a coffee while Lindy sipped a diet Coke.

"Where's your car?" I asked, with a hint of guilt in my voice. I liked anonymity in my food forays.

"We always park around back, so folks can't keep tabs on us." Lindy said with her mouth full. "The doughnut jokes are more than we can handle."

"Can we get together this weekend? My boss told me I don't need to be back until Monday." During my visit at the clinic, I had decided to resolve at least a few of my concerns regarding Sarang. Still I'd need a break at some point.

Her brow furrowed. "Come over for dinner tomorrow night," she said, cramming a donut into her mouth. The voice from the radio on her shoulder rattled off a series of numbers, apparently directing her to an accident on the highway.

I followed them out in time to watch the two squad cars peel from the back parking lot. It reminded me that I needed to call Snake.

"Aquilae," he said, in his macho cop voice.

"You with someone?" I asked, never wanting to be one of those needy ex-wives.

"Just a sec," he said. I assumed he was finding a suitable place to talk. In a minute he said, "Hey, I'm glad you called."

"Where are you?"

"I'm at Henne-thieves."

I cringed, knowing this would cost him. This is the store where cops buy new uniforms, bulletproof vests, and associated police gear. The name is Hennessey's, but their prices warrant the nickname.

He correctly interpreted my silence. "The agency has a policy for replacement uniforms," he said by way of explanation.

"I thought mustard would just wash out." I went for the jugular. Then I realized my mistake. "You don't wear a uniform."

"I needed a new vest."

My heart stopped for an instant. His wasn't the kind of vest worn as part of a three-piece suit. His was the kind that stops bullets and knives. Needing a new one meant only one of two things. He'd gained a ton of weight in a week, or he'd taken a hit.

"Did you gain weight?" I was trying to keep it light.

He ignored the jab. He's always had more self-control than I have.

"Do you want to know or not?" The carrot and the stick. He was good.

I hated to give in, but I really did want to know why he needed a new bulletproof vest.

"Okay, Eddie, why do you need a new vest?"

"Got bit."

My heart stopped. "Dog or dirt-bagger?" I had to ask. One was worse than the other was.

"K-9 took the closure off," he said laughing. "All I got was a scratch on my finger. We were competing for the same perp."

"Good thing it was you instead of a guy afraid of dogs." I knew some people would have coded out.

"Yeah," Snake said. "They told me there was a guy who left the Honolulu Police Department for some little department without K-9s after he lost the toss with one of the dogs. Guy got bit as a kid—afraid of dogs—always has been." Then he paused. "I have to admit, it was pretty scary. Gunther really likes his work."

"How's Gunther?" I asked in my talking-to-the-dog-voice, so sugary and nice that I missed something important.

"He let go once he tasted cop instead of bad guy."

"Yeah, I'd do the same. Did you get treated?" I asked, just in case he might be glossing over something serious.

"Yeah, sure." Mr. Casual.

"What'd you do, suck your finger?"

"No," he paused, "I had the fire department do that."

"Ew!" Not the answer I expected. Law enforcement and fire fighters have an unwritten animosity. The cops said they'd be as popular as fire-fighters if they didn't give tickets. Fire fighters just sit in their recliners and say they're better looking. Deep down there might be mutual respect, but on the surface it was all bad-mouthing and smack talk.

"Just kidding," he said. "I only had a scratch."

Somehow, I didn't believe him, but before I could say as much he said, "I gotta go."

This was the story of us. I had to go. He had to go. Unfortunately, we had always gone in different directions. Before I could say goodbye, he was gone. I didn't even have time to tell him about my latest findings.

The day was growing late and I wanted to hurry back to Sarang's for a meal and a nice long walk with Wharf. What I didn't expect was the greeting I got from Sarang when I arrived.

As we got out of the car, in a flash, Wharf dashed between my legs, then, raced around me nipping and grabbing at my hands. With each pass, I could feel the soft inside of his mouth, though teeth never met my flesh. Snake could take a lesson. As he bounded around the car, the looseness of his jowls was counter-balanced by the flight of his ears. I had to laugh. That act alone helped me to realize the importance of this beast in my life.

Sarang peered through the screen door, watching the Wharf Show. Even through the screen, I could see my sister's grimace. Although I had a guilty conscience, I chose to disregard my previous discussion with her about the pot. Neither did I mention my talk with Dr. Pease. Sometimes it was easier and less painful to ignore the conflicts.

Sarang said, "Let's go surf."

Hell yeah, that's exactly what I needed to clear my head and my conscience! "Okay, I need to change." We left the pooches in the house. A few miles down the hill, we headed toward the beach in Buffy and turned at the familiar road to the dump. There were few cars in the parking lot. As we watched the waves, we could see the break switching from a right to a left. The waves were collapsing inward instead of curling. It left nowhere to drop in about half the time and a great opportunity to get your arm broken. We paddled out anyway.

From the ocean, the fire-scorched earth was visible. I imagined the line between the ancient Kula lava flows and the younger more fluid Hana flows. I could see random rubber trees in the near distance, relics of a turn-of-the-century entrepreneurial foray into the latex business. This agricultural venture, like the subsequent pineapple and sugar cane plantations near the center of the island, had died at the hand of cheaper labor and lesser regulations in other parts of the world. It made me worry again about the *taro*.

In my daydreaming, I missed a wave that Sarang opportunistically paddled to and caught. As I watched her surf, she looked normal, healthy and happy. I turned and paddled back into position. I realized hers was a profoundly solitary illness, one from which the rest of the world is excluded, as the person dealing with it is further isolated from solutions.

On the horizon, I saw a nearly imperceptible lift of the ocean. Ah, I had a clean set coming my way. I waited. Patience is one of my least abundant attributes. I waited through the first small wave as a local *moke* on my right paddled in and caught it with a trashed little short board. I waited past the second wave that a little kid with an even smaller board grabbed in a flash.

Then I took my time as the third in the set built up. I paddled to match its speed, then, popped up with my right arm flung behind me for balance and my left hand grasping to catch an invisible towline. By shifting my balance, I cut a hard right and slid down the face. Again, and again, I worked the wave's long curl into the beach where I dropped to my stomach and rode the foam to the sand, my head now blessedly clear of smoke and confusion for the first time in a week. Some surf sessions aren't so much full of adrenaline, but instead free from stress.

"That wore me out," Sarang said shortly after we arrived back at the cabin. "I need to go lie down. Could you turn off the sprinklers and shut everything down for the night?" With a nod, she closed the door to her bedroom. Under the door, I could see the light go on next to her bed.

Usually, I packed plenty of reading material with me when I travel, but not this time. Fortunately, one cabin wall was lined with books of every kind—bird watching guides next to thrillers, autographed best sellers shared shelves with worn classics, all mixed with tomes on Hawaiian culture and garden journals. Searching for the right book on these shelves was like a walk down memory lane for me. My gaze stopped on the center shelf, where the newest titles seemed to congregate at eye level.

I could see that Sarang had been doing her own research on coping. She also had several textbooks on psychology. I smiled at her fortitude in finding the most current and accurate information on her illness. It was also nice to know that Sarang was becoming her own advocate, especially as I had lost faith in Dr. Pease.

Next to the medical books was a small cloth-bound book with a silk-screened title on the spine that said simply, "*Poi.*" Its hand-made appearance was invitation enough for me to pull it from the shelf and take it to the worn leather couch. The book appeared to be one of a very limited edition, printed only six months earlier. The inscription, other than the words, "To Sarang" was unintelligible to me because it was in Hawaiian. It seemed someone had a remarkable command of the old language.

The only phrase that struck my memory was the word *Uila,* which I'd seen in the council meeting minutes. In the book, it said the literal translation means lightning. It said the word described phenomenon that the early Polynesians did not have names for: electricity, generator, battery, power line, and electric lights.

When Hawaiian members of the council grumbled about the power crisis, inevitably they referenced the word *uila*. Words that honor lightening as an act of Nature in their lives revile the form of the hydroelectric power that threatened their primary source of sustenance and tradition—the *taro*. I thought I had heard the same words earlier when I was leaving the Hunt Goldwaithe's media circus. I doubted it was coincidence.

No fan of poetry, I usually shied away from books of verse, but I felt compelled to read this one. By its very nature, it was a piece of handicraft nearly lost. I had seen only a few hand-printed and bound books in my entire life. I was curious as to where this one would lead me.

To Wharf at my side, I said, "At least it's written in English." For its modest size—seven by ten inches and less than a half an inch thick—it obviously contained much effort.

Wharf now lay fully sprawled, with his head resting in my lap. I held the book with one hand and stroked his big velvety ears with the other. Only the reds of his eyes showed. As I turned each page, a half-moon of white would gaze at me then disappear once I resumed stroking. With a little grunting noise, he stretched and rolled over onto his back, all four legs spread-eagled in the air. My heart made a little breaking move. I couldn't imagine why anyone would suggest Wharf was mean, dangerous, or racist for that matter. It simply was not in his DNA.

I read the stories and poems slowly, savoring each word like a piece of chocolate. This book, this piece of art, was a story of the Hawaiians regaining their local lands, told completely with metaphors, word pictures and analogies. By the end, I could see that the book had set a future direction for the community to follow.

Thumbing back through the textured pages, looking at the block print illustrations, I wondered who was responsible for the work. Nothing told of who developed, edited, and constructed the book. Near the inscription to Sarang, were the numbers 3/11 written in pencil. Was this a date or simply the number of volumes produced?

After turning out the light, I listened to Wharf's breathing as I watched the stars. When Sarang's light went out, I settled down to dream about surfing. In jarring contrast there was a phone ringing in my dream. Although I answered it in my dream, it kept ringing. Like cold honey, I slowly poured myself off the couch in a stupor. It was light outside, but the atmosphere still held the scent of night's presence. What kind of idiot would call this early? My voice sounded like a growl when I said, "Hello."

"Where were you last night?" Lindy sounded like she'd been up for hours and had knocked back her tenth cup of double espresso. I wondered how we could be friends. We really had nothing in common.

"I was here reading."

"Then why do you sound hung over? Need a little hair of the dog that bit you?"

Her joke reminded me of Snake's dog bite story. I looked around for the others, but apparently, Sarang was already outside with the pooches. "Too late. Either the dogs are out for a walk, or I ate them in my sleep."

Lindy laughed and then apologized. "Sorry to wake you. I thought you'd be up by now. Do you still want to meet for dinner tonight?" As though a treat for acquiescing she said, "I'll introduce you to my boyfriend."

"I'm looking forward to it. What can I bring and what time shall I come?"

"Bring yourself and Wharf. We still don't have any pets but we've been talking about a dog. It'll be good for us to see yours in action. How about dinner at six? We're not exactly night owls."

Every time she used the words, "we" and "our" I could hear pride in Lindy's voice. It sounded like she was finally in a steady, sane relationship.

Chapter Twenty-One

I spent the rest of the morning helping my sister in the garden. By noon, I thought I'd have heatstroke if I didn't rest. Even Wharf, who had dogged my footsteps for four hours, looked spent. We both longed for water, internal or external. Sarang had more stamina for gardening than surfing. The herb garden needed constant weeding. It was a wonder that my sister could keep it up, since her garden kept expanding.

"Sarang, let's go down to Māko's for lunch. I'm pooped." I didn't need to ask twice.

On the way, we witnessed a steady stream of traffic, a mix of tourists and locals returning to historic Hana.

Among the locals, certain groups met at Māko's on a regular, if informal basis. The coffee club, whose participants had probably come and gone at least once already this morning, were huddled around two tables in a corner. They considered themselves the arbiters of society in Hana. In reality, they knew a great deal about each other's lives, but were not dialed in to anyone else's. Nor did they care.

Near the door sat several women on their lunch break from the *taro* farm.

As usual, Cowboy Roy sat at the counter conferring with Māko between orders. Apparently, the quick-mart business was solid enough to afford employees, and Roy enjoyed that success. Sarang pulled out a chair from a table in the middle of the restaurant, and I agreed to the location without comment.

"You two gonna to make me wait on you?" Ruth asked slapping plastic-covered menus on the table, as she passed by with four of the all-day breakfast specials for the two surfers seated near the windows. They hardly muttered a "thank-you" before digging into their double orders of white rice, scrambled eggs and Portuguese sausage platters.

On her return, she poured water with one hand and patted Sarang's back with the other. Ruth was all business. "Our special today is fried Spam. You can have it with fried rice or homemade garlic linguini." Māko's specials were always unique combinations. Without a second thought, I ordered the special with the linguini. I had all day to let the garlic wear off before going to Lindy's. Sarang ordered the same and we guzzled water in the few minutes it took for the plate lunches to arrive.

"I wouldn't order Spam at any other restaurant, that's for sure," I said as I savored the mystery meat. Sliced and pan-fried as hot as possible for a minute, it was crunchy on the outside and soft, moist and tender on the inside.

"Even at home I wouldn't order this," I said between bites of aromatic linguini. I kept eating until I noticed the look on Sarang's face.

"Are you okay?" My sister sat still, transfixed. "Sarang! What's wrong?"

Snapping back with a blink of her eyelids, Sarang asked, "What?"

"You were in a daze. I thought something was wrong with you."

"Oh, it kind of surprised me when you talked about 'home.' I still think of this as your home."

There it was. The issue I had battled for years. Was this home anymore? What defined home? Things, people, and places were not as stationary for us as they were for others. We were military brats and then military ourselves.

"Sarang, I am one of the few people here who is originally from Hawai'i. Even the legislators are from out-of-state. Let's just say I'm at home in Hawai'i." Not much of a reassurance, but it would have to do. Fortunately,

Roy was approaching our table. I knew that he would change the subject.

"You two women too good to sit at the counter now?" Instead of a teasing tone, his voice sounded hurt. Before I could say a word in response, Sarang said, "Go away, Roy." She did this without a glance in his direction.

"SARANG!" His voice boomed.

Again, quietly, but this time looking him directly in the eyes, Sarang said, "Go away, Roy." Like a well-mannered dog, he did as commanded, leaving the restaurant without another word, his eyes downcast. He slammed the screen door.

Before I could ask what had happened, Sarang said, "Let's go sit at the counter." She moved her lunch without waiting for a response from me.

I hadn't a clue what had just taken place, but rather than face off with Sarang again, I decided to visit Roy this weekend. I knew he would tell me the whole story. In a small community, tempers and personalities clash, with and without great provocation. Usually the issue becomes lost in time and life goes on. I suspected that this was a case of two sometimes-bitter pills battling for sport or habit.

My self-explanation was interrupted by shouts from one of the surfers. His buddy was losing his breakfast back onto the table. Everyone in the room fought the gag reflex to join him. It took just seconds to determine the cause of his discomfort, as the shouts of "Call 911!" erupted.

The surfer pointed to the limp, bloody body of Cowboy Roy in the middle of the street.

I ran to the door and glanced both ways before dashing to his body. In that instant, I saw a red pickup rounding the curve toward town, but it was a blur. When I checked for Roy's pulse, there was none.

His shoes had been knocked off his feet by the force of the impact and one bone protruded through his skin. His face, hands, and clothes were shredded. Despite the blood, I checked his airway and began giving him

CPR. I heard and knew that my replacements were on their way as sirens closed the distance. After a few breaths, I added chest compressions and kept at it until the ambulance arrived.

Everyone from the restaurant and the clerk from Roy's store had gathered at the side of the street. I stepped aside as the EMTs took over, and within seconds, the ambulance sped away, just as Haspin pulled up in his patrol car. He looked at the pool of blood and the two shoes, then said, "Anyone see what happened here?"

The people standing around dissipated like morning fog as the sun rises. In an instant, only Haspin and I remained in silence at the edge of the street. No one had seen who hit Roy. Sarang sobbed as she and Ruth returned to the restaurant, holding each other up on the way.

"I ran out as soon as I saw him in the street," I said. "I saw a red pickup heading that way." I pointed toward town. "I checked his airway and began CPR, but never got a pulse." Although trained in body recovery and investigation, giving CPR to a friend's devastated body had left me breathless and weak. My lips were cut and stinging from the force I used.

"According to my radio," Haspin said, "the paramedics revived him in the ambulance. He's in the hospital now, but no word on his injuries yet."

I hadn't realized I'd been holding my breath. With a big whoosh, I felt the world's weight lift from my shoulders. Maybe I'd made a difference... I had kept his blood moving long enough. Saving lives was not easy.

"I can't believe we don't have one witness," Haspin said.

"Me neither." I saw my sister and aunt huddled on the cafe porch and joined them.

"Ruth, Sarang?" Both women were crying. This was not a comforting sight. I wanted them strong and immortal. "Haspin said they got Roy's heart started on the way to the hospital." Before I could say more, Sarang headed toward the parking lot. At the bottom of the steps, she stopped and looked around, as though lost.

"Where's my car?" Sarang voice was weak. She was in shock. At the same moment, my aunt and I realized she was at a tipping point. One we weren't sure we knew how to handle.

"Aloha, can you drive us down to the hospital?" Ruth asked. "I'll go tell Māko we're leaving."

As we sped to the emergency room, I sensed this accident was significant. I hadn't seen Sarang and Ruth fall apart like this since Frank had died.

At the hospital, the admitting nurse gave us little information.

"They only speak with family members in these cases," I said. "Otherwise outsiders would spread the word before the family found out the details. I can respect that." My little speech out of the way, I went off in search of a diet soda.

Returning to the front desk, the same nurse directed me to the emergency room waiting area, where I found Ruth. "Where's Sarang?" I asked, as I tried to get comfortable on an old Naughahyde chair.

"She's with the doctor." Ruth wouldn't meet my gaze.

"Ruth, how'd she get to speak with the doctor?"

Ruth mumbled a response—just like in the cartoons when a character slips the bad news out the side of his or her mouth—as though that will help. I had to ask again, this time speaking slowly, while I locked onto Ruth's eyes.

"How did she get to speak with the doctor?"

"She told him they're getting married." The information thundered through my soul once it reached my brain. Sarang lied and said she was engaged to Roy! "And the doc believed her?" If the situation weren't so dire, I'd have laughed.

Ruth wasn't laughing.

"Are they really?" I asked.

Ruth nodded.

"Why didn't she tell me?" Ever the child, I focused on myself.

"She thought you wouldn't come home if you knew she had someone to help her. She wanted to tell you in person, but ever since you got here, you've been working or fighting. That's why Roy stormed out this morning—he wanted to tell you then. Sarang blames herself for his injuries."

I wondered at my own intelligence, if not my sensitivity. I had assumed that Sarang was content being alone. It seems I had assumed many things based on my own self-centeredness.

My fear about Roy's health escalated in proportion to my guilt. How could I be so blind to things right in front of me? Sarang had never taken every meal at Māko's. In order to see each other while I was in town, she and Roy had been meeting in a neutral setting. Now he was lying in intensive care.

This time my tears flowed freely, though I remained silent. I stared at the ceiling, hoping to avoid eye contact, even with Ruth. Still I cried. After a few minutes, the well ran dry. I left the waiting room to wash my face.

By the time I finally found a restroom, I was completely lost. I seemed to be in the hospital's administrative area. Hard to believe a hospital this size needed a full layer of administration, but apparently, it did. The room labeled 'Records' emitted a pattern of light into the hall. Assuming I could get directions inside, I tapped on the door and entered. The immaculate filing system with color-coded folders filled the shelves. On a table in the middle was a scanner. I looked like the hospital was in the process of transferring its files storage from paper to digital.

On the shelves, I took a second look at one section where there were several folders as thick as encyclopedias. Curiosity overwhelmed me as I pulled one to see why that that particular patient warranted a book. I knew it was wrong, but I couldn't help myself.

The pages inside were yellowed and faded; yet, the label appeared new. The last name on the file was Smith, the first name, Melanie. The patient's treatments hadn't been lengthy, just frequent, with a series of mysterious maladies covering about five years. Then the entries ended. The dates on the file were almost thirty years old.

The name Michael was on the next file and the name Madelaine on the third. It reminded me of the Nooners with their Hawaiian god names. It seemed like this family had stuck with the same first letter for each kid. Before I could compare the files to see if all three had had the same illnesses—for no good reason other than I was nosey and trying to avoid reality—a clerk walked in and gasped.

"Can I help you?" Though her words were civil, her body language said, "What the hell are you doing in here?"

"I got lost. I thought someone in here could tell me how to find the restroom or get back to the emergency room." I lowered my hands from the files and brushed a tab onto the floor. When the nurse stepped forward to retrieve it, I saw that it marked a missing file. The reference was to a file changed from the last name Kila to Smith. That struck me as odd.

Kila had been Mallory's maiden name.

Chapter Twenty-Two

Upon my return, Sarang and Ruth were thumbing through magazines, that mindless turning of pages without reading or focusing. They both looked drained.

I sat down and embraced my sister. "How's Roy?" I asked.

"He's alive. The doctor said you saved him by keeping up the CPR until the paramedics arrived. He's in surgery now, but they're not sure of all the complications. It looks like he fell before he was hit. There's a lot of damage to one leg. Thank God, the truck didn't strike him while he was walking—they said he wouldn't have survived that."

Ruth stood. "I'm going to find a toilet. You two talk."

"I should have told you the truth right away," Sarang said, "But I didn't want to upset you on your first trip home. Then things kept getting in the way. There was never a good time to tell you about Roy."

"Why would it upset me that you were planning to get married?"

"Well, just because we used to make fun of him for being kind of a reprobate when he came back from Desert Storm."

"Sarang, we were a lot younger then. And we didn't know what war meant."

She looked down.

"There's more?" I asked.

"Plus, I wasn't sure how you'd feel about him being Samoan."

That one hit me hard. My second accusation of bigotry in the same week. A criminal accused me of racism because he's dark-skinned and now my sister was doing the same because her fiancé was Samoan.

I thought about it. I think of myself as Hawaiian, even though I'm blonde. I figure birthplace trumps hair color. The guy I'd arrested at Mala Wharf seemed to disagree. Sarang obviously assumed that I related so much to the *haole* community that I wouldn't approve of her new husband, even though I'd bailed on the whole community after a white woman sold nude pictures of me with a Hawaiian man. If I had room in my head for an additional ounce of introspection, I might have used it. At this point, I was simply on overload. Not an answer in sight, I hid out in the past.

Sarang and I began recalling stories about Roy from our youth and Ruth joined in. By the time a doctor came out, six hours had passed. He was pleased that we seemed in good spirits. It would help us to face the news he carried. "Sarang, may I speak with you privately?" He spoke in soft tones.

"We're the only ones in here now. You can tell all of us." She referred to Ruthie and me.

The veteran surgeon sat atop the magazine-littered coffee table facing us. We were like See No Evil, Speak No Evil, and Hear No Evil. He focused on Sarang.

"Roy is stable now. His heart stoppage was due to shock. The problem is with his legs. The fracture was so severe that it took us this entire time to try to piece it together. The bones that punctured the skin are a real concern because of the strong potential for infection. He's doped up on pain meds, and he's getting plenty of antibiotics. The problem is that I'm concerned about the healing process. If we get an infection, we may have to amputate his right leg."

Sometimes life really sucks.

What I wanted to know was who hit him and why they didn't stop. Ruth called Māko with the news. From him the information would filter throughout the community.

When I finally checked the time, I realized I was late for dinner at Lindy's. The doctor told Sarang that she could stay in the room with Roy, and handed her off to a nurse's aide to help her settle in. This left me with the task of bringing Sarang some clothes and toiletry items and of caring for our dogs.

"Sarang, I'll go get your things and be right back," I said.

"You're supposed to be at Lindy's tonight—go there and then bring over my things. There's nothing much to do until Roy wakes up."

"No, I want to be here with you."

As soon as I said it, Sarang showed even more signs of fatigue and stress.

"Please, Aloha. Just do as I ask. Come back later."

Ruth nodded and ushered me from the room.

"Don't be hurt Aloha. Sarang needs to be alone with him for a while." She hugged me and said, "She loves you."

After calling Lindy and giving her the headline on why I was not coming for dinner, despite Sarang's protestations, I drove to her *hale* in the lingering sunlight.

The dogs barked and hopped around the car as I drove up the driveway. Stinger allowed me to pet her briefly. Wharf, on the other hand, let me know how lonely he had been without his human companion. Sensing my sadness, he covered me with warm, wet kisses and wagged his tail as he followed me around the cabin. His presence was calming.

While I had packed up my sister's bag, the sun had set and the resulting shadows demanded headlights. During this round trip, I had seen at least five more red pickup trucks. What's with the plethora of red trucks in Hana? I thought back to my arrival, with Kū behind me at the roadblock. Then there was the diver with the red pickup when Lindy and I did our second dive at the dam. Now it looked like a red truck had hit Roy. I almost forgot the one that Lono Nooner's girlfriend had parked at the clinic.

I pulled into the hospital parking lot and noticed several pale green vehicles illuminated by the huge light poles. They belonged either to the Park Service or to people who had purchased them through government surplus auctions.

The co-op also had its own fleet of vehicles. They were all red.

Duh! Mystery solved.

Again, as the hospital smell assaulted my nostrils, I recalled Nate saying that Mallory was sick all the time, like those patients with the thick files in the hospital storeroom. That whole family was diseased. I wondered how they were related and why the name Kila had been switched to Smith. My mind bumbled along.

Once in the Critical Care Unit, I saw Sarang walking with a nurse back to the waiting area.

"How's Roy doing?" I asked. Sarang looked wrung out. Hoping to cheer my sister, I added, "I brought Stinger to see you."

Sarang smiled, and then said, "He's pretty out of it, but at least he's not in pain right now." She and I talked as we walked arm-in-arm to the parking lot where Stinger yelped frantically at the sight of Sarang. Between Wharf and Stinger, it sounded like coyotes had invaded the lot.

After several minutes of scratching and petting, Sarang forced Stinger back into my car.

"Thank you for bringing her down. I think everything is going to be okay."

Not much reassurance, but still I appreciated it. I watched her walk back into the hospital—from my perspective—a tall woman looking smaller by the minute.

I was distracted during my drive back to the darkened cabin. Out of the car, I hardly noticed the dogs, as I searched for the key hidden outside the front door. Normally I wouldn't have locked it, but with no one around, I decided to secure it while I was gone. The key was tough to find in the dark.

Then I realized it shouldn't be dark since I'd left the porch light on when I left. Annoyed, I reached up to pull out the burnt out bulb, only to have it flicker on with my touch. I tightened it back into the socket and pushed on the cabin door. It was already unlocked.

Since I hated flailing around for light switches in the dark, I'd left the light on above the stove. However, it was pitch black inside the cabin, too. Outside, the remaining trees creaked and swayed in the wind. I had an uncomfortable feeling.

With one hand, I reached out to find the light switch. Instantly I remembered that because of the cabin's single-wall construction they had opted for plug-in lamps around the room's perimeter. I would need to grope around and turn one on. After bumping my leg on an end table, I found the first one. Cursing, I twisted the switch, and the pale yellow light erased the darkness. As I returned to close the door, I could hear Wharf growling on the porch.

I dug around in my bag for my handgun.

Where was Stinger? "Wharf," I whispered. He was sitting on the porch steps. He didn't turn his head in response to his name. Instead, a low growl continued to emanate from deep within his chest.

I could hear something crashing through the brush by the driveway—probably the Chow chasing a chicken. Loudly, I called Stinger, who instantly appeared at the base of the steps. Okay, so maybe a deer was working its way through the forest. I'd heard guys were flying them in from Lanai to create hunting opportunities. It was a classic case of human intervention upsetting the balance of nature.

Then the dogs' growls escalated to barks. I tried to stop them as they both took off after the noise. I was sure I heard someone say, "Ruh-roh" like Scooby Doo being caught by Old Man Smithers.

With gun in hand, I followed the sound of their barking as I ran down the driveway. A vehicle started just as I got to the road. It pulled out of a blocked access driveway about a hundred feet away. The silhouettes of two crazed canines chasing it were visible against the taillights. Even at that distance, I was almost sure it was another damn red pickup truck.

I called the dogs back and together we retraced my path up the driveway. In my rush, I had left the cabin door ajar. Now, still holding my gun and with the dogs at my side, I searched the interior, even looking in the closets and under the bed.

Whoever had been here had left everything in place, even Sarang's pot that I found stashed in the pump house. When she asked me to pack up her things for a night at the hospital, I included the brownies she had baked earlier in the day. Sarang told me that the brownies, laced with pot, eased the nausea created by the antianxiety meds.

Still, rattled, I remained fully clothed, locked the door, and kept the dogs inside. Since nothing was disturbed, I tried to settle down to sleep.

That's when I realized the handmade book was missing. Why would anyone break into a locked house for a book? It must have been someone that Sarang knew, since they found the key. Why had they turned out the lights and run away? No matter what the reason, it made me uneasy that someone had been prowling the cabin.

Still, I needed to sleep and I did. I was out within fifteen minutes, but I slept in fits and starts. Finally, as dawn broke, I settled into a deep slumber. It wasn't until late morning that the ringing telephone woke me. It seemed like the sound of a phone had become my new alarm clock.

Sarang sounded strong despite having spent the night in the hospital with Roy and a killer dose of stress.

"How's everything going?" All barriers were down and we had recaptured the closeness we both treasured.

"We had a little excitement here last night," I said, letting Sarang absorb the statement before I continued. "It seems that someone wanted in your cabin. He, or she," I added, now trying to be perfectly politically correct, "was leaving as I got here. Want to tell me what that was about?"

I could hear Sarang sigh over the phone. "I thought you were going to Lindy's. How was I to know you'd lock the door? Kāne came rushing in here last night saying you nearly shot him!"

Funny how some people overreact when they're guilty. "I didn't even point my gun, let alone fire a shot. I might have been scared, but I'm not stupid. If I ever point my pistol at someone, it won't be a feint. I'll shoot if I need to." Then I stopped my mini-rant and changed focus.

"Did you get the brownies?" I thought I deserved some credit for being her mule. It seemed like every time I turned around I was doing something to risk my second job.

I noticed that Sarang didn't refer to marijuana as dope, which was probably just as well. The active agent in the marijuana is THC—tetrahydrocanibol. It would be nice if my sister could take it in the prescribed form of Marinol. However, it was probably best for Sarang to feel part of the treatment, even if that meant growing a little pot in the backyard and baking funny brownies.

I laughed aloud. Leave it to my special sister to have to break the law to stay in the game.

While listening to Sarang's update on Roy, someone knocked on the door. The dogs broke into a chorus of barks and growls. They really needed to work on their timing. Bark earlier. Through the window, I spied a red pickup truck. I ended my call with Sarang, promising to be at the hospital within an hour.

When I opened the door, I shuddered. What next?

Chapter Twenty-Three

"Nate, what are you doing here?" My stomach was turning somersaults.

"I needed to talk with someone. We used to be best friends. I thought maybe we still were." Nate looked sorrowful.

"Uh, I was just leaving." Fortunately, I had slept in my shorts and T-shirt from the night before and had just crawled off the couch.

"I should have called first." He hesitated at the door.

Once the pressure was off, I realized I wanted to ask him some questions. His intentions seemed honorable, even if my questions were not.

"Come on in while I finish getting ready." I opened the door for him. "Can I get you anything?

"Had a double shot on the way up," he responded in coffee-talk. He paced around the cabin as he spoke. "I need somebody to talk to who wasn't completely taken in by Mallory. Now that she's dead, it's like she was a saint."

I was surprised, but before I could comment, Nate said, "I don't want to be mean but I'm really mixed-up." He stared vacantly out the wood-framed door.

"So, do you ever dive anymore?" I asked.

"You know I don't dive. I've got asthma."

"That's weird. I thought somebody told me you were doing underwater photography."

"I bought a used underwater camera to take pictures of Missy when she was learning to swim. It didn't last long, though, because she was always sick. Then she got cancer. I didn't even know what happened to the equipment until last week."

183

"It must have been hard for you to have both Mallory and Missy sick so often."

"It was at first, but when Missy got worse, Mallory got better. It was almost a relief when the leukemia was diagnosed—at least then we knew what we were fighting." He sounded almost nonchalant.

"What about Mallory's mom? Did she help much?" I still pictured that woman at the cemetery.

"They took Missy to a faith healer—a nice guy, but it didn't help. It got her mom together with Pastor Toby, so Betty can lean on him. Mallory was the fourth child she'd lost." His eyes welled up again, as his emotions simmered close to the surface.

Before I could ask another question, the dogs stepped between us. Wharf sat upright, mild, yet attentive. Stinger faced Nate and snarled. Her stance was pure malice. Then Wharf looked him directly in the eyes, which was not a good sign. I ushered the dogs out the front door, leaving the screen closed so we could keep an eye on each other.

I had been a horrible host: brushing my hair and teeth, feeding the dogs, and getting ready to leave as soon as I had all the information I needed from him. If he wanted a true friend, he'd be wise to look elsewhere. I no longer felt I owed him a thing. He wasn't my problem with Hana.

"Why did you put Mallory's photo in the paper?" His voice rose in volume. "Aloha, why did you do that to me?"

"Nate, that wasn't my fault. Nagasako's did it and I don't know why. I'd never allow a shot like that to get to the media. That's why I want to know what their problem is with me." My tone was sharp.

Nate looked...sheepish? Then he said, "Haven't you heard of Daphne Spence?"

"The news chippie?" I asked, wondering what she had to do with this topic.

"Their daughter," he said.

"What! You mean Dee Dee Nagasako. From school?"

"Yeah, well she changed her look and her name after those shots of you and Brother helped her make the big time. She followed the story to Los Angeles. You made her famous and now she's too good for this town. Her parents blame you. If you hadn't been screwing Brother Love to death, she might not be famous, and they wouldn't have lost their daughter to the mainland."

The dogs were back at the screen door and I let them in. I was trying not to lose my temper. Screwing Brother Love to death! Where did he get his information?

Before I could respond, Nate rolled farther down the slippery slope. "I guess I'm just lucky that I hooked up with her on her first and only trip home. As soon as everything is settled here, I'm moving to LA to be with Daphne." Nate said the last part with an unpleasant grin.

His look, plus the tone of his voice, was enough for the fur ninja. Stinger and Wharf both growled. I nearly laughed aloud. Nate lowered his voice and held his hands palms-out. If he had been a dog, he'd have rolled over and shown his belly.

"Nate, you dumped me like a hot rock when Brother died." Then I muttered, "So much for the truth, or for loyalty." With each statement, I snapped my fingers, emphasizing how quickly he had moved away from me and into Mallory's arms. "So let me set the record straight—I was a nude model, that's all. I thought you and I loved each other. I never had anything more than respect and friendship with Brother. So despite your deviant little thoughts, he did not die in my arms."

Nate finally got to the point of his visit. "Daphne would actually like to get some shots of you and the dog for her story on police profiling. We heard you'd targeted a guy on Maui this week. Her new show is all about righting injustice."

All the little back-talking personalities in my mind went silent. This was a first. Then, they banded together. I was ready to leave the cabin and was more than ready for Nate to leave. I needed to get away before I hurt someone, even with words. When the telephone rang this time, I was relieved. The dispatcher from the police department said I needed to come to their office immediately. I wondered what strings Haspin wanted to pull now.

"I'm sorry that you lost Missy," I said to Nate. "I'm sorry you lost Mallory. I'm thrilled that you dumped me. I deserved better than you offered. Now I'm leaving. You can do the same, or stay here with Stinger. Your choice."

I loaded my bags into the car and looked at Sarang's cabin. It was nice to have this home to revisit, but I wanted to go home to Lahaina. "And, no, I won't give an interview on the guy I arrested this week. Neither will my dog."

Wharf and Stinger left Nate on the porch still staring at us as they jumped in my car. I'd bring her home later. I backed around and left the cabin, much the same as I had found it upon my arrival. I still had some hurt, but it wouldn't keep me away again for years.

Covered with a thick coat of dust and road debris, Nate's red truck had no signs of damage or even a minor impact with a human. Replaying Roy's accident in my mind, I was desperate to discover who had injured my newest family member, so I motored down to the cop shop in search of answers.

Stinger, on the other hand, had curled into a tight ball on the passenger seat after having called doggie shotgun. Like a charcoal-colored caterpillar, her fur resembled crushed velvet with her little pig-style tail laying relaxed, leaving a divot of compressed fur on her rump. Not something you'd want to mention if you spoke dog, since Sarang had told me Stinger has a hair-trigger temper on a bad day and is generally snarfy the rest of the time. Apparently, she has the neighborhood cats and feral chickens on her permanent hit list, along with all Mynah birds, geckos and squeaky toys. You can tell just by looking at her that Stinger swears like a doggie dockworker, but probably has a heart tattoo that says "Mommy" somewhere under her fur coat.

"Is Haspin in?" I was proud of my self-control. I'd asked to see him without a sneer and I didn't call him Dog.

"Nope. This is his day off. Would you like to speak with someone else?"

"Is Dhong here?"

"You bet. I'll let him know you're here. Aloha Jones, right?"

Now I was impressed. This guy even remembered my name. I honored him with a smile while he called into Dhong's office. Suddenly, after feeling the ugly duckling around Nate, I fluffed my psychological feathers to resume the presence of a swan. Amazing what a kind word and a smile can do for a person's attitude.

By the time I was in Dhong's office, I was the professional investigator again, completely at ease with my own skills and responsibilities. All the inner personalities had calmed and were quieting playing Go Fish.

"Good morning, Chief Dhong. Thank you for seeing me. I hope I'm not interrupting you too much."

He was closing a file drawer as I entered, so I knew that I had intruded on his time, but he gave me a smile of welcome.

"It's no problem, Aloha. After all, I did request that you come down. And call me Lon."

"I thought it was Haspin who wanted to see me."

"That's partly why I asked you to come down. Did you happen to tell anyone that you'd be here?"

I didn't like the sound of this. "I assumed it had something to do with me sticking my nose into your investigations."

"Not at all Aloha. I'm happy to have your help. I was on the phone yesterday talking about your skills with Babs McKee."

Uh-oh! He knew my boss. I blushed and looked at my feet. Haspin had called to check up on me—now Dhong, too? Before I could comment, Dhong laughed at my sheepish look.

"Yeah, Babs and I go way back. She sure thinks a lot of you. I'd like to hear any thoughts you might have on this case." The tall man was leaning back in his chair with his hands clasped behind his head.

"Which case? And why did you call my boss?"

"The murder of Mallory Kila Deems."

The voices in my head did a little cheer. My instincts were correct. Mallory's death wasn't an accident.

"Now we're talking," I said.

"Yeah, but before we talk any more I need to know about your loyalties."

"What about my loyalties?"

"Aren't you and Lindy old friends?"

"What's that have to do with my work? Don't tell me *you're* after her, too."

"Who did I say was after her?" Dhong's face registered puzzlement.

"No one, I simply witnessed Haspin in action."

"Hmm, I didn't know that was still going on. If you think this department is a mess, you're right."

Dhong sat up and slid an open file folder toward me. In it was a photo contact sheet. "Whose idea was it to make the second dive?" Somehow, Dhong made it sound like a bad idea instead of good police work.

"It was my idea. I saw what looked like a lens cap impression on the autopsy photos of Mallory's body. I had a hunch that we'd find a camera that might give us a better idea of why she had been diving at the dam. I would have gone with or without Lindy."

I felt tiny beads of sweat forming at the base of my ponytail.

"This thumb drive has the shots that came from that camera."

In a glance, I knew he was wrong. My look at him said as much.

"Yeah, I, even I know there are no kelp beds behind the dam. These were shot in cold water." I confirmed as I wiped the trickle of sweat from my neck.

"According to Nate, they did own an underwater camera. He said that it already had pictures on it of their daughter."

I doubted that, and asked, "How can you be sure he's telling the truth?"

"Good question." Dhong handed me a police report dated only a few days earlier, which documented a police call to a domestic dispute at the Deems' residence. An underwater camera was the cause of the ruckus.

"Deems threatened that he'd 'kill her' if she lost the camera."

I could see at the bottom of the sheet that the result of the police call was a 'No Contact Order' between the warring parties. Attached were the developed photographs from the camera. The little girl in them splashed water in delight at her experience. I recognized Missy immediately.

Dhong watched me as I read, then said, "That's why he wouldn't come to the dam to identify her body. He thought we were trying to set him up to violate the 'No Contact'."

At that, Dhong chuckled. "There are more paranoid complaints and conspiracy theories around here than there are people to investigate them."

"Before we go any farther," I said, "is there a problem with the chain-of-evidence?" Given that my photo of Mallory made the local newspaper's front page, I thought I knew the answer. However, Dhong's response still surprised me.

"Yeah, you could say that, but that's the least of my problems."

"It's Haspin isn't it?" I said, thinking he was gunning for me.

Dhong stopped smiling and said, "Yep, Haspin wants this desk."

I laughed, but stopped when I saw the look he gave me.

"Even though I agree with you as far as his qualifications," he said, "I'm an elected official. Every four years I face a challenger. Doesn't matter if that person is a *moke* or not, if the folks like 'em. Me, I kind of like the process—forces the constituency to think and to talk. I like the feedback."

"But, there's no election this year." Even I knew this.

"That's why he's trying to have me removed from office."

I frowned. The coroner was the only person who could impeach a chief.

"No," I shook my head, side-to-side, in disbelief.

"I'm afraid so. I heard through the grapevine that Gommer is planning to relieve me from duty and appoint Haspin as my replacement."

"How? Why?"

"Apparently, he's planning to 'respect my privacy' and not divulge any details publicly, other than to say that I'm guilty of malfeasance."

"That could mean anything from impropriety to criminal wrong-doing." I should have stopped talking right then, but I didn't. "It leaves people thinking things are worse than they are." Gulp.

"I made the same assumption. Then I contacted Babs for advice. That's where you come in. Babs suggested that until I get this resolved, someone from outside this department should handle the dive investigation. Your name came up."

Therefore, he didn't trust his own force. "I can see why you don't trust Haspin. I wouldn't either, but Lindy wouldn't work against you." Even as I said it, I wondered. After all, it seemed she'd been harassed on-the-job. She might be disgruntled at the non-support the system was providing.

"How long since you've spent much time with Lindy?"

"It's been years."

"A lot's changed here in Hana. New folks moving in. A few locals have also changed... dramatically. Lindy's boyfriend is involved in politics—letters to the editor, disruption of public meetings, crazy signs up in the yard. That doesn't mean she's part of the problem, but I can't be sure."

"Chief, I'm sorry, but I can't help you. I'm heading home today. I'm on administrative leave because of a bogus racial profiling complaint. Moreover, Cowboy Roy was run over last night. If I was going to chase after something it would be that."

"How about we make a deal? I'll tell you what's happening on Roy's case and you help me on the Deems murder investigation. From what Babs said, she can manage without you for another couple days." He paused, "And you're right. At this point you don't really have a job to go back to."

I didn't notice the look on his face. I felt like I was deciding if I wanted to take the mission from Mr. Phelps. All I needed was an audio tape to disappear in a cloud of smoke to seal the deal.

Instead, I just nodded and Dhong handed me a second file. A juvenile named Nono Nooner had been booked on charges of vehicular assault and grand theft. He must be Lono's son.

Dhong made my end of the deal easy to fulfill. I knew where I needed to go, a place I should have visited two days earlier. I had one stop to make first.

Chapter Twenty-Four

I drove to the hospital and parked in a nice shady spot, leaving the windows lowered for the dogs. The morning was still cool and clear, but I wasn't sure how long I would be gone. Once inside, my first stop was the records room. Fortunately, it was a Saturday and no office staff seemed around.

I jimmied the door and forced the lock.

After confirming my own suspicions and *not* calling Dhong with an update, since I had actually violated a wealth of privacy laws, I hustled to the Psych Department. Dr. Pease was not in, so I walked on to Intensive Care, where the nurse told me Roy had been moved to a regular care ward. This was incredibly good news.

Sarang and Roy had already charmed the hospital staff. As I left the nursing station, I overheard the nurses comparing anecdotes about the couple. I was happy that my sister again had a partner in her life.

"Tell Aloha, Vee'll be bock!" Great… I recognized my dad's voice as he did his "famous" Arnold impersonation, thinking he's the only one who does it.

I stopped just shy of a turn in the hall. I heard my parents walking in the other direction. I wanted to see them, but I needed to finish my deal with Dhong, first.

Before I could speak, from behind me Sarang said, "You're leaving, aren't you?"

"I had been planning on it when I left the cabin this morning. Now I'm not sure when I'll go."

"I know you, Aloha," she said. "Couldn't you stay one more day?" The look in Sarang's eyes was one of pure love.

"I'll be back again soon."

Sarang knew that I was telling the truth. Some of my demons were gone. "Tell the folks I'm sorry I missed them."

It was true. My parents, Ike and Eve, as we sisters often called them in lieu of Mom and Dad, were a riot, if by riot you meant riot. Colorful, outrageous, emboldened, loud and filled with energy, they let little slow them down. Right now, as much as I loved them, I couldn't afford the distraction.

Dr. Pease walked toward us. "Oh, sorry," he said as he did a little head bob that I recognized as his body language for *I wish I was invisible*. "Hope I'm not interrupting." He saw the tears in the Sarang's eyes.

"What's up?" I asked, thinking of how Snake told me his Mexican auntie struggled when learning to speak English and she couldn't get the difference between "what's up" and "up yours." I felt the same way about Pease.

"As long as my favorite patient is here, I thought I'd check on how you're all doing." Dr. Pease said, as he opened Roy's door and waved us in. Again, as we passed close to him I thought I smelled alcohol, this time the scent of when it's oozing from your skin after a serious bender.

"Gee, I thought Missy was your favorite patient."

He shot me a look that I couldn't interpret.

"I enjoy all my patients, but it was difficult to lose Missy."

"Well, Missy was special wasn't she? Too bad she didn't carry your name along with your DNA."

Pease didn't exactly squirm, but he closed the door and said, "Miss Jones, do you have something to say to me?"

"I guess I do, Dr. Pease. Would you like to discuss it here or in your office?" Sarang and Roy were wide-eyed.

To me, he said, "Let's go to my office." To Sarang he said, "I'll check in with you later."

I had goose bumps on my arms as we walked the quiet halls to his office. He closed the door gently and the cold click ran the goose bumps down my legs. From his desk, I picked up the framed photograph that I had noticed earlier in the week.

"Missy was you daughter wasn't she?"

He did the head-bob thing again and slumped down into his chair, a man defeated.

"At least your diagnosis of her was accurate. Too bad you can't say the same about Mallory."

Pease stared at me, his brows scrunched together, confused. Then he said, "It wasn't Mallory, it was her mom. I eventually figured it out, but by then, it was too late. It took me years to find a way to help. Still, I was too late for her, too."

Now I felt confused.

"That's why you're here isn't it?" he said. "Gommer said he'd pressure me until I opted not to run for coroner. Did he send you? Why hassle me now? He won."

"I'm not here because Gommer sent me. I figured it out once Nate told me how Missy's chemotherapy treatment required the Leucovorin rescue. Nate told me she had died suddenly while he and Mallory were working. At the funeral I could see that Betty enjoyed being in the spotlight. I figure she just didn't give her granddaughter the antidote to the chemo."

After a brief pause I added, "I also saw some files in the storeroom that helped with the puzzle."

At this, Dr. Pease gave me a sharp look. "You got a warrant to look at their files?"

I chose to ignore his question and ask my own instead. "How did

Gommer make you pull your application?"

"He's blackmailing me." Dr. Pease had bigger problems than finding out how I had gotten my information. "I had signed up for an advanced forensic pathology course so I could run against him as coroner in the next election. He should have pulled the blood tests on Missy. If he'd been doing his job, her grandmother would be in jail today. Instead, he wrote it as an attended death, which didn't require an autopsy. I confronted him, saying that I would go after his job. Then he accused me of raping or coercing Mallory and some other things. The statute of limitations had expired, and it *was* consensual sex. Even if I'd won that battle, I would have lost the election."

"Dr. Pease..."

"Call me David." For a doctor, this was the same as an army dropping its last line of defense.

"Was Mallory pregnant by you when she died?"

"Oh, God, no," he whispered. "I begged her not to have any more children. I couldn't bear to see it happen again, and I know her mother. The best I could have done was criminal prosecution if it happened again, but another man would have lost a child."

As an afterthought, he added, "But, no, the child wasn't mine. For all I know, Mallory could have done it the next time. It goes that way you know." Then he added, using the disease's acronym, "With MSBP," referring to Munchausen's Syndrome-By-Proxy.

"Dr. Pease," I said, allowing him his title, "You were a victim, too, in the sense that they took advantage of your caring nature. Missy's blood type didn't match Nate's. You donated blood for her transfusion. I'm surprised the whole hospital didn't know."

"Between Mallory and me, we kept the files private. I would have married her." He started weeping. "I loved her and wanted to do the right thing." He should have grabbed a tissue but he didn't. Instead, he just let the tears and snot run off his face. "She I said I was too old."

I hated to dump on him further, but I needed my own house in order before I could leave Hana.

"Doctor, I'd like you to refer my sister to someone else. I'm sure you've been doing your best, but ... " I guess I didn't need to say anything else. He just nodded. Then he said, "My dad was right."

I looked at him.

"Never fool around with someone unless they have more to lose than you."

Weird fatherly advice, I thought. Probably better than I ever got, but still weird.

I returned to find my sister reading aloud to Roy, who had his eyes closed. Very cute. The little stone in my chest felt like it could burst with either happiness or sadness. I hugged Sarang.

"Aloha, what was that about? Where's Dr. Pease?" she whispered.

"I'm sorry, Sarang. I asked him to remove himself from your case. You know how I always think I have some dread disease. I guess it's a way to get attention. It's just one of my many failings." Sarang gave me a stern look.

"Okay, well, one of my few failings. Anyway, I found out that I am not really a hypochondriac; I just have a good imagination and a few unfounded fears. Some people get so much attention from being ill that they take it several steps farther. They have Munchausen's Syndrome."

Roy opened his eyes for a second and then they fluttered shut. They had him on some good stuff.

I continued my explanation, "Munchausen's patients go past hypochondria, which has real symptoms, to creating their own symptoms. They do all kinds of things to make themselves ill. It is completely untreatable and darn hard to diagnose. In some cases, they create illness in others—Munchausen's Syndrome-By-Proxy, or MSBP. It passes from one generation to the next, like abuse."

I could see Sarang processing the idea, putting the puzzle pieces together edges first and working toward the center.

"I ended up in the records room yesterday. I found out a lot about the illnesses of Betty Kila's children."

"Children, what children? There was only Mallory," Sarang said.

Roy stirred, opened his eyes and slurred, "Joan of Arc wasn't married to Noah."

Uh-oh. Roy was starting to make sense to me. I nodded.

I saw Sarang put in place what I thought was the last piece in the puzzle. "The last Hono'māele Ridge Fire? That was thirty years ago."

Sarang did the storyteller thing again. It was like watching Madame Zadora gear up for a fortune.

"She—Betty—had been living up there and then her kids were killed in the fire. Everyone thought it had started with a lightning strike..."

"Only metaphorically," I said.

She beamed at Roy. "I told you she'd have to solve something while she was here."

I hated being talked about as though I was not in the room and suspected Sarang was doing this on purpose. "You do realize that I am still here. At least for the moment."

Sarang said, "Please stay." Roy grinned, with his eyes shut. He was good. We practically glowed with familial love. A Kodak moment? Nope, more of a Prozac moment.

"I gotta go." I blushed. "Sarang, you know I love you. And, you too, Roy. It's been quite a week." I paused. "Sorry. It's just that..." I had some kind of blockage in my throat, probably a tumor, and I knew I'd start crying if I tried to explain my receding bitter feelings.

Sarang changed the subject to let me recover my composure. "What'll happen to Dr. Pease?"

"I don't know and don't care." Distracted at the thought, I picked up my bag. Now it was time to see who had killed Mallory.

"Roy, get well and take care of Sarang for me. Oh, I almost forgot, Stinger's in the car. Where should I take her?"

"Leave her with Ruth. Tell her I'll probably need a ride home tonight," Sarang said. "Let's see. How about eight? Do you think eight's too late?" I knew Sarang didn't want me to leave, so she was drawing out the instructions.

"I'll be back soon. Let me know if you two need anything. After all, I only live a few hours away." Really, it was only about 70 miles from Lahaina to Hana. I hugged them both.

At the car I said, "Okay kids, we're going on a treasure hunt." Stinger and Wharf hung their heads out the open windows, their ears—and in Wharf's case —jowls, flapping in the breeze. Wharf rode shotgun.

Somebody had to know why Mallory had been diving.

I had forgotten to ask Sarang why Kāne had come to her cabin the previous evening and why he had taken the little book. I planned to call her before reaching my final destination.

In the meantime, at Māko's, a flood of questions greeted me.

"How's Roy? Did they find out who hit him? Is Sarang okay? Are you okay?"

The gossips had been busy. I answered everyone's questions, remembering to thank each one for the concern. I knew they would work together to help support Sarang and Roy through the coming months of tough rehabilitation.

When I finally called the hospital, the ward nurse told me that both were dozing. I didn't want her to wake them. Maybe Ruth would know why Kāne had been at Sarang's cabin and snagged the book.

When asked, her answer didn't surprise me. I was on the right track.

With a quick goodbye to Ruth and Māko, I darted to the parking lot where Wharf and Stinger were snuggled together on the back seat. When I opened the door, they both gave me plenty of wet kisses. I never thought I'd feel bad about leaving Stinger, but the old girl had surprised me.

Reverting to my old habit of conversing with animals, I said, "I'm glad they have you to keep them company." To Wharf I said, "We better be careful or we won't be able to leave this old snaggletooth."

I handed Stinger off to Ruth and drove to the Hana *taro* farm to see Kāwika Padriac for a lead on finding Lono. I didn't know where the other brothers worked, so this was my only clue. Plus, I was delighted to see Kāwika again.

"Well, hello. Two visits, this must be a record." As he said this, I blushed. To tease me further, he added, "You're not stalking me are you? I heard you'd been asking about me."

At this comment, I turned crimson. Only one way to keep him from discovering that the idea had crossed my mind.

"You caught me. I'm madly in love with you… and I was just hoping you'd notice."

Then I gave him my best come-hither look. It was Kāwika's turn to blush when I said, "Wishful thinking?"

Raising his hands in surrender, he said, "I give up."

"Is Lono in today?" I brushed an errant hair back around my ear.

"No. Do you want me to find someone else?"

"Does he still stay up at his mom's place?"

Again, he engaged me in flirtatious banter.

"Well, I wouldn't tell just anyone, but I guess I can make an exception for you—since you're stalking me and everything."

I had always fantasized about having a relationship with Kāwika, but it never took. I realized I wasn't interested anymore. Snake was just too good. I only needed one man and he was it.

Kāwika seemed to sense the mood change. He still smiled, though this time somewhat wistfully and said, "He still lives up at his mom's place."

"Thanks Kāwika. I gotta go."

This was becoming my standard exit line. I wrote my home number on my card and handed it to him. "I might not be available at the work number. If you ever get to Lahaina, give me a call." Then I winked.

Oh yeah, I could still flirt.

It was only as I climbed into my vehicle that I saw my glowing face in the mirror. I still had a dusting of cinnamon sugar at the edge of my mouth from the malasadas snack I'd pilfered at Māko's. Aagh, I am doomed to flirting purgatory!

I was still fuming at my social interaction debacle when I arrived at the Nooner compound. I snapped out of my snit when I saw Lindy's squad car already there.

The Nooner family home had grown from a single unfinished rambler, still sided with tarpaper, to a compound. Between the shacks, tattered plastic tarps, and junk cars, the yard area had a dull litter of dried mud puddles and battered kids' toys. I left my car running, and shoved my Glock into my back pocket as I stomped up to the front porch. Before I could knock, someone opened the door.

"What are you doing here?" Lindy asked. She held the door close to her body so I couldn't see inside.

"I could ask you the same thing." I said, confused.

"Gee, did you learn that questioning technique at the academy or from television?"

Sheesh, she wasn't killing me with kindness. Guess I was back in trouble.

I heard a male voice from behind her. "Well, Lindy, it looks like your friend will help us after all."

This was not what I had hoped to hear. I wanted Dhong to be wrong about Lindy. This time I would need to eat crow. Well, if I had the chance.

Kanaloa stepped out, grabbed my wrist, twisted my arm behind my back, grabbed my gun and put it in his pocket. Lindy handcuffed me. I needed to stall, if for no other reason than to come up with a plan. My internal voice chanted: *Dive your plan, plan your dive.* I'd broken the cardinal rule. I hadn't planned this well.

Chapter Twenty-Five

"Lindy, what's going on? I came up here looking for Lono and you cuff me. Let's cool off and talk about this."

"Sure Aloha, we can talk in the car. The guys can follow us in your rig." She grabbed my neck and jerked me over to her squad car. Kāne hopped in a red pickup and pulled out first. I had heard them tell him to go to the hospital. My only hope was Wharf, but I could see him wagging his tail at Kanaloa, Kū and Lindy as they climbed into Buffy. They were feeding him powdered donuts!

I didn't speak until they pulled onto the paved highway, heading toward the dam on the plantation side.

"Guess you're not taking me to the police station, huh?"

"That's the bad news." Lindy said. "The good news is that you get to go diving again. Remember, once you told me that you hoped you'd die underwater?" She didn't do an evil chuckle, but I got the idea.

"Lindy, we've known each other forever. I don't want to sound stupid, but I thought we had a special friendship." Lindy grimaced at me.

"Good guess, Aloha. You've always had your whole family, although you were too stupid to appreciate it. Then you killed my father, and now, I am going to even the score. The best part is that I get to kill two birds with one stone."

She smiled. I didn't smile back. We were approaching Māko's, probably the only place I could cause a problem and not have the Nooners beat me into compliance.

Lindy's radio squawked a rapid series of numbers. She lifted the mic to respond. "Good news, now I'm the only one on duty. Haspin just signed out for lunch. Your timing was perfect."

As they drove past the restaurant, I could see Māko behind the counter. I willed him to look up and see me, but he didn't. Apparently, my telepathy skills were crap.

We reached the dam in a few minutes. Without my gun, and with no backup plan, my mind raced first through solutions, followed immediately by an awareness of insurmountable problems. I went back to Lindy's earlier statement.

"What do you mean, I killed your father?"

Lindy turned off the car and said, "You're such a douche. My dad was Brother Love. You remember him—or was he just another ship in the night for you?"

"Yeah right, and who was your mother, Queen Elizabeth?" Lindy was delusional. Maybe I could talk reason to the Nooner boys.

"You should be able to figure that out. After all, my adoptive parents started my name, Melinda, with an "M" like all the others. Little did they know I'd end up going to school with my sister?"

The resemblance began to appear, like trying to find Waldo. You can't see him until someone points him out, and then you can't see anything else. Mallory Kila Deems was Lindy's half sister. Mallory started school late and was a year older. Suddenly I thought my own parents weren't so quirky after all.

We had reached the dam. Lindy held me as we watched Kanaloa pulled my dive gear from Buffy's trunk.

"Put your gear on." They could have asked me this all day without compliance, but they had Wharf on a leash, still feeding him donuts. Additionally, Kanaloa held my Glock to his head while Kū had me in his sights. Once they removed the cuffs, I compliantly struggled into my wetsuit.

"Here's the plan, Aloha. You get to do what Mallory screwed up the other night—slightly disable the dam." Kū brought out the drawings I'd seen the evening I performed the body recovery and said. "She was as bad a diver as she was in bed."

I looked up at him and said, "Did you see her on the video cam?"

"That's right. I had to shove my fingers down my throat to puke so that my shock would be believable. Good old Garrison played his part well, too." They all laughed. Seeing the shocked expression on my face, he said, "No, Daniels didn't have anything to do with it. He's just an old man acting like an old woman, worried about everything, but nothing important."

On the drawings, they showed me where I would dive—they were making me swim into the turbine.

"We were going to do this with Mallory, but she decided to be a secret agent chick instead. Like we really needed photos of the welds."

"Why are you doing this? Why would you send your girlfriend to die?" To Lindy I said, "Mallory was your only sister. My God, are you both out of your minds?"

"She wasn't exactly anyone's girlfriend," Kanaloa said. "She wanted attention and we gave it to her. We'd never make her part of our plan. She was white. And as for why? When the turbine is opened up for repairs, we'll pack it with calcium carbide, just add water, a spark, and ka-boom!"

Garlic—that's the scent in calcium carbide, hence the smell in Mallory's tank! Calcium carbide and water together equal acetylene gas. The dam repairs would be needed to remove my dead body from the turbine. I started to feel clammy.

"Aloha, you're white, too," Lindy said, "So you might not understand. This is the only way we can reopen the rivers for the *taro*. We will no longer be held hostage by the government." Together the group said in unison, "Uila."

How could people interpret so differently the same book?

Then they stabbed a hole in my BCD with my dive knife. Punctured, there was no way I could use it to stay on the surface. They threw the knife far out into the reservoir, and pushed me into the water. It seemed a lot colder than it had before. The icy trickles, like cold champagne bubbles, invaded my wetsuit at the ankles, wrists, and neck.

Kū strung a line around my arms and legs to give me the appearance of an accidental drowning, just in case I didn't go through the turbine.

"Kanaloa, if you blow up the dam, it will destroy the farm. What about the *taro*?"

Like an automaton, he recited the problems with genetically modified *taro* that I had read about in the local council meeting minutes. "Reduced genetic diversity, altered nutrition, overuse of food sources, and they displace the native plants."

"Disabling one turbine won't solve the problem." My voice was becoming shrill.

"When this dam goes," Kū said, "it'll create a domino effect. We'll have water spilling all the way to the ocean. The last straw was when the Feds set their 'controlled burn' and blamed the fires on lightning."

As the water topped my wetsuit, I clenched my regulator in my mouth. With no air in my BCD, I had to walk along the bottom as they pulled me forward. Lindy had drained the air from my scuba tank until there was just less than 500 psi remaining. They gave me ten minutes to be pulled into the turbine, or drown. My incentive was the gun they held to Wharf's head. If I didn't comply, they told me Sarang would be next. I believed them.

Their calculations were good on my air consumption. Their assumption that I would die for Wharf was even valid. However, I had a different plan, and I was scared. If my plan didn't work, it would simply look like I had followed Mallory's example and broken the first rule of diving. Dive your plan and plan your dive. Even Dhong knew that I would have gone alone on the last dive if Lindy hadn't joined me. I couldn't dwell on that. Survival would take all my experience, confidence and concentration.

I moved toward the gushing underwater entrance to the turbines as quickly as possible. Anyone who's ever tried to jog in a swimming pool knows the energy it takes to speed along without fins. With the various lines tangled around me, and my inability to achieve neutral buoyancy due to the empty BCD and twenty-pounds of lead, I had few choices.

Seconds, and then minutes, passed in a blur. I kept watch on my pressure gauge, relieved to see that I could control my air consumption despite the frantic situation. When I reached the base of the giant retaining wall, I began the difficult chore of peeling off my gear. To make my plan work, I had to become streamlined and neutral.

I used the tiny spare knife I kept in my BCD pocket to cut the various lines wound around me. While taking off my equipment, I set my tank on the bottom. I would take a deep breath from it then slowly empty my lungs while I worked. This too was in preparation for my plan. I was deliberately hyperventilating, trying to find the right level of oxygen in my body —somewhere between super-oxygenation and passing out—not an exact science.

My last task before pushing the equipment under a rocky ledge was to don my fins. It was nearly impossible to let go of my scuba gear. Without it, I knew I would die. But without risking my plan, I would die. It was a do or die situation.

I took a final pull from the air cylinder, pushed it down, and prayed I wouldn't be drawn into the current. Then I pushed my gear, with the ropes attached, into the turbine entrance.

They say there are no atheists in a foxhole. I was ready for divine intervention. It looked like the water gods had heard my prayer as I saw the gear recede into the darkness.

Only then did I push off the wall's concrete edge. With my mask and snorkel still in place, I swam upward. The daylight helped slightly with the visibility, but mostly I listened for the sound of flowing water.

In what seemed like an eternity, but in reality was only a few seconds, I clutched the rods across the opening to the overflow valve and the tunnel from which I had recovered Mallory's body. I had exhaled slightly during my partial ascent, and at this point, I released even more air from my lungs. With my level of body fat and full lungs, I would still have been too buoyant for my plan to work.

The current caused me to shoot through the opening without further preparation. Just as with Mallory, the moving water's force pulled off my fins. I thought I would glide down the chute, but instead, I tumbled.

The roar of water was deafening in one ear and neutral in the other. They hadn't pulled out my hearing aid so another one bit the dust. Partway down, the water's sound got even louder; the turbines had stopped.

Lindy and the Nooners would be gone, with the exception of Kū who was probably on his way down to the control room to "lend a hand." I had time only to considered Wharf's fate before I blacked out.

Chapter Twenty-Six

Sirens intruded on my hazy dream. I had my eyes open, but my vision and hearing were blurry. Next came the overwhelming desire to vomit, which I did. The contents of my stomach caught in a tiny whirlpool and flushed themselves down the stream. Again, my senses went on the blink. In another moment, I bobbed to the surface.

I heard sirens punctuated by a deep, low, familiar howl. I wanted to call out, but I didn't have enough air in my lungs to whisper, let alone shout.

I slipped back underwater, this time sinking several feet. My own natural ability to float was failing against the strength of the undercurrents. I was so cold I couldn't feel my wounds or the grasp of Wharf's mouth around my wrist. I blacked out again.

The next words I heard were, "Looks like we're too late."

When Haspin reached down to check my carotid artery for a pulse, I threw up on him. He half carried, half dragged me to his squad car, and pushed me into the back seat. Wharf, soaking wet, plopped himself onto me, creating a proverbial dog pile.

We reached the emergency room in less than four minutes. Haspin later told me I stopped breathing twice. I gave out completely as soon as the orderlies placed me, stark naked, on a gurney.

I woke up four hours later to voices arguing in the corridor. I shivered and tried to reach for a blanket only to discover that I was already covered with a thin, warm, air blanket. Even the air I inhaled, through a breathing tube, was heated. I could taste the plastic in my mouth. Someone reached out and rubbed my arm through the covers. Again, I slept.

As seemed inevitable on this journey, again a ringing telephone brought me to consciousness. I tried to sit up to answer it. I was surprised to see that Chief Dhong was sitting next to my bed. This was one strange dream.

"I'm not in Kansas, am I?" Comprehension slowly registered on his face.

"You're not in the Midwest at all, though I do appreciate your getting into the middle of my investigation. Don't worry, we'll talk tomorrow."

Then he patted my arm and left the room.

When I awoke again, Māko, Ruth, Sarang and Dhong stood nearby. Roy was lying in the bed next to me.

"How sweet," I said, "We're sharing a room. Do we get a reduced rate?"

"They're charging us extra for the dog bed," Sarang said.

Wharf stood, stretched, and then pushed his nose up under my hand.

"Am I the last one to know how this all turned out?" I said.

"Well, it's not like you told us that you'd decided to solve it yourself," Roy said from his adjacent perch.

"Hey, how did Haspin know how to find me?"

Everyone laughed, and then Māko said, "As you know, Haspin's a bit overzealous about his job... on several levels. Even though it was his lunch break, he'd been cruising around hassling tourists and scaring jaywalkers. Lucky for you, there was a report of a rabid dog on the plantation side of the dam. Lindy called in to say she had it covered, but Haspin was just looking for a chance to get her alone. By the time he pulled up, Wharf had jumped into the water after you."

I looked at Sarang. "I thought Kāne would hurt you."

"Kāne's okay." Sarang spoke with sadness in her voice. "He's been trying to sort out which side he's on for a long time. When Lindy handcuffed you up at their place, he realized he could live better as a Hawaiian out of jail than in. He was calling me at about the same time Haspin found you."

Dhong spoke next. "With his help, we arrested Kū and Kanaloa. I wasn't looking forward to a Ruby Ridge standoff here in Hana."

"Well, you already had the kid in custody," Roy said. "I recognized him from coming into the store, even before he hit me."

"What kid?" I was very confused.

"Andi Arnold's son," Babs said. "They planned have him run me down to get you off the diving investigation. It served two purposes for the Nooners. They told him that it was his initiation into the family. Given their feelings about whites, I doubt they would have ever bailed him out."

Dhong rose to leave.

"I guess you get out of here this weekend. You tell Babs that if she doesn't treat you right, I'll hire you away from her."

He smiled and left.

I hesitated for a moment and then said, "Sarang, I thought you might be involved in the plan to blow up the dam, too—what with the book and your feelings about the *taro*."

"You should have been worried, but not for that reason. I helped them to publish the book. I thought that if I could bring them into the discussion that," she looked to the heavens, "we could channel their emotions and energy. Instead, they used us to legitimize their actions and recruit others."

"What about Brother being Lindy's father?" I asked. It made me shudder to think that my fallen idol was not only my ex-best friend's dad, but also Mallory's.

"Before Betty moved here, as you discovered, she had three sick children; two died in a fire. The dog saved the baby. Betty told the authorities she was too traumatized to raise Melinda, and put her up for adoption. Lindy's new, and I might say improved, parents brought her to Hana hoping she would have the best of both worlds and shortened her name from

Melinda to Lindy. Unfortunately, she had too much of her mother's mental illness in her. In this case, nature overwhelmed nurture."

My fuzzy little brain puzzled, "I'm surprised she started all her kids' name with an M instead of a B."

Ruth answered this one. "Betty is short for Margaret."

Just then, my hero walked, or more accurately, ran into the room. Just like when Snake thought I was about to be shot by the big guy on the beach, he came in looking for trouble. Sometimes that old Alpha male can get himself a little too worked up. Were it not for the crowd, I think he might have cried.

What were we going to do?

As Wharf and I eased out of town in the Mustang, I looked back at the valley, including both sides of the river. The view was spectacular, despite the blackened ridges.

I hoped that the runoff from those areas wouldn't ruin the streams. I was certain that the *taro* farms wouldn't go the way of the dinosaurs, but they needed all the help they could get. Disabling the dam and returning the river to its natural course had seemed the only solution to some—but they were deluded dreamers seeking glory, not solutions.

Remembering my pup in the backseat, I commented to him about the absurdity of Lindy and the Nooner brothers, Lono excluded. Tragically, Kanaloa, named after the god of procreation had impregnated Mallory between break-ups with Lindy. To eliminate the threat to her twisted psyche she was more than willing to participate in Mallory's murder. Kū, after the head injury was an easily manipulated soul trying to belong with his brothers. Kāne had been on the fence, embracing the theories and conspiracies right until it came to killing me, Sarang's sister. And Lono, he was indeed alone in his desire to work within the system. The one son dedicated to producing *taro* for the Hawaiian people regardless of politics.

"Cripes, I'll bet they even had a secret handshake." Wharf moved to the front seat and raised his paw at the word shake.

"You're such a smart baby-dog," I said, and then I smooched him behind his downy ears, making a kissing and then a low growling sound.

"Mom loves you."

With that, we motored along the 600 turns back to Lahaina.

A week after I got home, I received two manila envelopes in the mail on the same day. The first I opened was from Dr. Pease. Based on notes from his father's medical and psychiatric efforts with Margaret Kila, he informed me about the issues that had killed his daughter. I think sharing the information with me was a way for him to work a part of his twelve-step program.

> Dear Aloha,
>
> As you know, everyone's parents are a little strange. Yet my father, a country doctor himself, could not have understood Betty's illness and the subsequent consequences on her children and my daughter.
>
> Miranda, the oldest, was by default the family's governing spirit. Although she had only seven summers on earth, she matured in dog years. Dark circles under her eyes lent her a constant appearance of sadness. Her pale skin, clear and lusterless, told her story. Being the oldest had stolen her childhood, with her mother a partner in crime.
>
> Sixteen months younger was Michael, who held Betty's internal conflict within his soul. He knew he didn't get enough love, but he didn't know why. The rage in his mind cast a constant shadow over his angelic face.

Melinda was the youngest. The daughter of a local kahuna, her complexion was darker than the others' skin. Betty saw the devil in this baby's bronze eyes, and she prayed to the god of the day for the child's death.

Betty was like the cow that bears a lovely calf, but lacks the innate ability to nurture. Certainly her own mother had cost her the self-respect and confidence that might allow even the most abused to survive. One thing Betty knew was that an overt exhibition of emotion was false. Never mentioned were the words commitment, compassion, or even heart-felt passion.

All those years ago in her most recent relationship before the fire, her boyfriend suggested that maybe the children were from Hell. Betty reflected on her children's wild habits and desires. Then she compared them to her own.

To Betty, it was not a choice. It was a commandment. While her children and their pets slept, she lit their home on fire. It was the best of solutions. The family dog rescued the youngest, your friend Lindy, who was quietly placed into foster care.

Betty was the ultimate survivor. She became prominent in our community as she wrapped the robe of martyrdom tightly around her grief-wracked shoulders. She immediately bore another child—Mallory, who in turn had Missy, my daughter. Her untreated illness prompted her to kill again by not giving Missy the rescue dose of medicine used to counteract a particularly lethal dose of chemotherapy.

My apologies for not righting these wrongs sooner.

David Pease

The second envelope was from the county. By-the-book Babs was notifying me by mail—as required by law—of the county terminating my employment. Although Wharf and I hadn't been found guilty of racial profiling—and subsequently not charged—we'd each exhibited "behavior unbecoming an officer." As a concession, the official notification said that Wharf could again become my personal property or remain with the county and suffer euthanasia. I felt lucky that I was just under-employed and not personally given the euthanasia option.

I gave Wharf a little pat on the butt and scratched his ears. Then I gave him the letter, which he promptly ate.

As Snake walked in the front door, Wharf ran to greet him with a big burp that spewed water and the noshed note onto the floor. Snake's new dog, Max raced up and bit Wharf's face in some kind of Chow police action. I ran to protect Wharf, slipped in the spew, and landed on my ass—a fitting metaphor for my day.